W9-DAP-543

The
Herbie Jones
Reader's Theater

The
Herbie Jones
Reader's Theater

DISCARD

by Suzy Kline

With illustrations by Richard Williams

J
812.5
K

G. P. PUTNAM'S SONS • *New York*

Text copyright © 1992 by Suzy Kline.
Illustrations copyright © 1985, 1986, 1987, 1988, 1992 by Richard Williams.
All rights reserved. This book, or parts thereof, may not be reproduced
in any form without permission in writing from the publisher.
G. P. Putnam's Sons, a division of The Putnam & Grosset Group,
200 Madison Avenue, New York, NY 10016.
Published simultaneously in Canada.
Printed in the United States of America.
Designed by Joy Taylor.
The text was set in Caledonia.

This book consists of dramatic adaptations of excerpts from books by
Suzy Kline, previously published by G. P. Putnam's Sons and illustrated by
Richard Williams. Most of the interior illustrations are taken from the original
books about Herbie Jones.

Permission is not required for classroom readings of the text of this book. For any
additional performance rights please contact G. P. Putnam's Sons.

Library of Congress Cataloging-in-Publication Data
Kline, Suzy.
The Herbie Jones reader's theater / by Suzy Kline : illustrated
by Richard Williams. p. cm.
"Consists of dramatic adaptations of excerpts from books by Suzy Kline,
previously published by G. P. Putnam's Sons and illustrated by
Richard Williams"—T.p. verso.
Summary: A collection of twenty-one episodes from four Herbie Jones
novels, adapted into scripts for reading aloud.
1. Children's plays, American. [1. Readers' theater. 2. Plays.]
I. Williams, Richard, date. ill. II. Title.
PS3561.L49H47 1992 812'.54—dc20 91-27347 CIP AC
ISBN 0-399-22120-4
10 9 8 7 6 5 4 3 2

To the schools and libraries
who participated in read-alouds from
The Herbie Jones Reader's Theater
during my sabbatical year 1990–1991.
Thank you for helping me with this project.

Acknowledgments

Special appreciation and thanks

To Margaret Frith, President of The Putnam & Grosset Group, who was enthusiastic about putting the Herbie Jones stories into a reader's theater.

To my editor, Anne O'Connell, for her thoughtful, hard work and fine-tuning of the scripts.

To Dr. Kay E. Print Janney, Professor of Drama at the University of Connecticut at Avery Point, for advising me on the role of narrator and how to move the action with the characters.

To the Torrington School Board for granting me a sabbatical to work on this project and the time to try it out in schools and libraries.

And to my husband, Rufus, for his helpful humor.

Contents

The
Herbie Jones
Reader's Theater

A Note to the Reader

A Friday night not so long ago, I was working late at my word processor when something strange happened. One of my main characters appeared on the screen!

"Annabelle Louisa Hodgekiss!" I said, squinting my eyes. "What are you doing?"

Annabelle smoothed a wrinkle in her yellow dress. "We wanted to talk to you."

"We?" Annabelle was the only character I could see.

"Psssst!" Annabelle whispered.

Now Herbie Jones and his best friend, Raymond Martin, were standing next to her. They were wearing white shirts, slacks, and their socks even matched.

"What's the formal occasion?" I asked.

Annabelle fluffed her hair. "I'll explain."

Ray rolled his eyeballs at Herbie. "She always has to be the boss," he whispered.

Annabelle ignored Raymond. "We wanted to ask you something," she continued.

"Yes?" I leaned forward. My nose was practically next to the screen. I wasn't used to talking to my main characters.

1

"We want you to put us in a reader's theater."

"What's that?"

"You make short plays out of our stories. Our readers could take our parts." Then Annabelle twirled. "Mine would be the best!"

Before I could say anything, Ray stepped forward. "Just a minute. My part is the funniest."

"Dumbest," Annabelle corrected.

"Stop arguing!" I said. "Herbie, what do you think of this? Do you want your stories to be read aloud like a play?"

Herbie smiled. "Yes! We'd be alive then! Someone would be reading the poems I write."

"They'd be cracking my great jokes." Ray grinned.

Annabelle beamed. "They'd know what it's like to be the best student in the class . . . ME!"

Herbie and Ray glared at Annabelle.

"Hmmm," I said, leaning back in my chair. "That's a lot of rewriting and work. I have other stories to think about. I'm in the middle of one right now."

Annabelle curtsied. "Please?"

Herbie bowed.

Ray stood on his head. "Pretty please?"

I shrugged. "I'd have to take a sabbatical to work on my playwriting."

Annabelle put her hands on her hips. "Suzy Kline, you've been teaching for sixteen years. It's time to spend a year just writing. This reader's theater project could be used in classrooms across the United States, and by families and friends who enjoy sharing a story aloud."

"Would you three be willing to help me out?" I asked.

Herbie took out his trusty notebook and pen.

"We're ready. What can we do?"

"Well, it would help if you brainstormed your favorite episodes," I said.

Annabelle looked over Herbie's shoulder. "Write down *Herbie Jones*. That's our first book. We want to go in order."

"Who says we have to go in order?" Ray objected.

"Hold on," Herbie said. "You two have to get along if we're going to help Suzy Kline. Annabelle doesn't have a bad idea. Let's start thinking of scenes from the first book and end up with the last."

Ray made a face.

"Hmmm, how about 'The Spelling Test'?" Herbie said, taking his pen off his ear.

"I'm hardly in that story at all," Ray complained. "I want 'Annabelle's Birthday Party'!"

Annabelle flared her nostrils. "HERBIE JONES, don't you dare include my birthday party. That's gross. Ray spoiled everything."

Herbie made a half smile. "Let's continue."

As the night wore on, my head dropped to the keyboard and I fell asleep. When I woke up in the morning, the screen was blank and my three characters were gone.

Quickly I read the printout that was on my desk:

— — — — — — — — — — — — — —

Dear Suzy Kline,

Here's the list of our favorite episodes. It wasn't easy. We only got as far as book four. Annabelle and Raymond couldn't agree on anything. My vote decided if we were going to use the episode or not. But, we finally did it, and now we're really excited.

Thanks for putting us in a reader's theater and making us feel more alive!
Love,

Herbie

Annabelle

RAYMOND

P.S. Annabelle says to plan on putting the other Herbie books in Volume Two.

— — — — — — — — — — — — — — —

As I shook my head and smiled, I put the letter aside and reached for the calendar. In neat letters I wrote, "Submit application for sabbatical for 1990–1991."

My characters had convinced me to do it.

Suzy Kline

About the Book

What is *The Herbie Jones Reader's Theater*?

Twenty-one favorite read-aloud scripts from the first four Herbie Jones books.

Who is it for?

For young and old who love to read aloud. For classrooms, families and friends. The scripts can even be read alone by an enthusiastic reader who loves to play different parts, or by two people who can alternate parts and read the entire script together.

How do you read it?

The Herbie Jones Reader's Theater is read, not memorized. The scripts are arranged in sequence and by book, but the familiar reader may want to pick out favorite scenes and read in any order.

When the reader knows the vocabulary and understands the directions inside the parentheses, he or she may want to work on using dramatic skills:

TIMING: Should I pause?

EXPRESSION: What's my mood?

GESTURES: What body language should I use?

EYE CONTACT: Am I looking at the person I'm talking to? If I'm talking to myself or I am the narrator, am I looking out at a "pretend" audience?

VOICE: Should I be loud, soft, or normal? Does the tone of my voice reflect my mood?

Why read it?

Because it's fun. Readers who take the parts of Herbie, Raymond, Annabelle and others make these characters and their stories come alive in a dramatic way. If readers try different roles—a boy taking a girl's part, or a girl taking a boy's part—they will come to understand the different points of view.

Who's Who

Herbie Jones

likes to read but he has been in the lowest reading group for most of his life. He carries a notebook, writes poems, reads books about spiders and enjoys teasing his older sister, Olivia. He hates doing skill sheets in his third-grade class at Laurel Woods Elementary School. Sometimes he uses his spy code number—Double 030—when he talks to his best friend, Raymond Martin, on the phone. Herbie cares what his parents think.

Raymond Martin

is in the lowest reading group in third grade. He loves Burger Paradise cheeseburgers, Bits O'Chicken, his dog, Shadow, and making foolproof plans with his buddy, Herbie. His spy code number is 992. He says he and Herbie are as tough as day-old donuts. He likes to draw Viking ships and act like a big shot.

Annabelle Louisa Hodgekiss

is the smartest girl in third grade. She is bossy and can be mean, but she works hard, is very neat and always obeys the rules. When she's angry with Herbie, she gives him the silent treatment or puts red checks after his name in her notepad. She's a good athlete and tries to be first in every contest. Her initials, ALH, are on most of her things.

Miss Pinkham

is a young third-grade teacher. She is fun, has a sense of humor and is an excellent diver. She likes early morning swims, liverwurst sandwiches and collecting ceramic owls. She keeps her basketball skills sharp by chucking scrap paper in the wastepaper basket after school. She and Herbie's uncle Dwight were classmates in high school.

Mr. Jones

is Herbie's father. He works the night shift at the local airplane factory and sleeps until two in the afternoon. He likes to fix things around the house and snack on SpaghettiOs. He hates dogs, noise and bills.

Mrs. Jones

is Herbie's mother. She works during the day at Dipping Donuts restaurant. She budgets her money, worries about her weight and usually forgets where she leaves her shoes. She likes to hug her children.

Olivia Jones

is Herbie's sister. She is an honor student at Laurel Woods Junior High. She loves English (and correcting Herbie), Lance Pellizini and her privacy. She does not like it when Herbie calls her Olive. To get even, she calls him Erb, after the hairy-looking seasonings people put on their salads.

Margie Sherman

is Annabelle's best friend. She is in the same reading group as Raymond. Sometimes she giggles and shrieks. Most of the time, she's kind. She's a good artist and likes to draw rainstorms and forked lightning.

John Greenweed

is the smartest boy in third grade. He has an asthma problem and sometimes has to go to the nurse for treatment. When he gets nervous, he fiddles with his empty inhalator. He loves cheese balls and going fishing with Phillip.

Phillip McDoogle

is John's best friend. He makes fun of Herbie and Ray a lot. Annabelle doesn't like him because he picks his nose. Sometimes he copies and cheats. He loves baseball and fishing.

Uncle Dwight

is Herbie's college-aged uncle. He plays varsity baseball, and during the summer when he stays with the Joneses in their attic, he coaches a baseball team at Laurel Woods Park. He's a little weird. He likes fried Twinkies for breakfast and talks to a monster ball. He's also sloppy.

Mrs. Hodgekiss

is Annabelle's mother. She has a flair for decorating. She prides herself on a neat house and loves to dine at the Grotto. She is president of the Laurel Woods Park Parents Club and works in the refreshment booth at the baseball games.

Mr. Hodgekiss

is Annabelle's father. He likes making eggplant parmigiana, watching Annabelle play baseball and cracking jokes. Annabelle doesn't think they're funny. Herbie does.

Shadow

is Raymond Martin's dog. He has fleas, sleeps in the doorway and once ate Ray's homework. His specialty is giving financial advice. His favorite dog food is Chucky Chow Bits.

The Monster Ball
(A non-speaking part that needs mention)

The Monster Ball is really a basketball. Uncle Dwight drew a monster face on it years ago with a permanent black magic marker. He says the Monster Ball knows everything. Sometimes when Herbie has a problem, Uncle Dwight asks the Monster Ball to help. Only Uncle Dwight can hear its voice.

Other Characters

Mr. Pellizini   is owner and cook at Dipping Donuts. He is proud of his restaurant and his son Lance Pellizini.

Mr. Bob   is custodian at Laurel Woods Elementary School. He works hard to keep it clean.

Mrs. Coffey   is head cook in the Laurel Woods Elementary School cafeteria. Her specialty is spaghetti and meatballs.

Sarah Sitwellington   is in Miss Pinkham's class.

Narrator   is like the stage manager. He or she establishes the setting, time and character motivation. When necessary, this person moves the action.

SFX Person   is the Sound Effects Person who makes special noises.

Other members of the Laurel Woods Community who have speaking parts:

Saleslady
Dipping Donuts customers
Policeman or Policewoman
Waitress
Minister
Umpire
Beechwood fielder
Beechwood pitcher

Part One

Herbie Jones

1

The Spelling Test

Characters: Narrator   Mr. Jones
              Herbie Jones   Olivia Jones
              Miss Pinkham   Annabelle Louisa Hodgekiss

Settings: Miss Pinkham's third-grade classroom; Herbie's house

Time: One week in March

NARRATOR: Herbie Jones sat at his desk and groaned.

HERBIE: I hate being an Apple!

NARRATOR: That was the name of the lowest reading group in Miss Pinkham's third-grade class. They were *still* reading in the red book—the one with the suitcase on the cover.

HERBIE: Miss Pinkham said these stories were about people going places. I don't think *our* group is going anywhere.

15

MISS PINKHAM: Herbie Jones! You were supposed to circle one answer for each question on your work sheet. You circled all of them. You *must* follow directions.

HERBIE: Yes, Miss Pinkham.

MISS PINKHAM: I'm stamping your paper with a monkey that says, "You can do better!"

NARRATOR: Monday morning was different though. Miss Pinkham went to the blackboard.

MISS PINKHAM: As a special bonus this week, I have a challenge for the *whole* class. If you can learn to spell your name, address, town, state and zip code correctly, I will mail you a postcard saying congratulations.

HERBIE: Hmmmmmmm, I know I usually don't study my spelling words, but . . . gee, that postcard would be good news for Dad to find in the mail.

NARRATOR: Herbie's dad works the night shift at an airplane factory and the first thing he does when he gets up around 2:00 P.M. is look in the mailbox.

HERBIE: I can hear him now . . .

MR. JONES: Bills! Bills! Bills! There's nothing but bills!

HERBIE: I can do something about that.

NARRATOR: As soon as Herbie got home that afternoon, he practiced writing his spelling words on the dusty coffee table. His sister Olivia was shocked.

OLIVIA: What *are* you doing?

HERBIE: Studying.

OLIVIA: Studying? Since when?

HERBIE: Since I got my spelling list. How do you study spelling?

OLIVIA: You're asking *my* advice about something?

HERBIE: Well, you do make better grades than I do.

OLIVIA: Herbie, *most* people make better grades than you do. (Clears her throat.) Well, Herbie, I write the words down . . .

HERBIE: Yeah?

OLIVIA: . . . and I say them to myself. That's about it. No biggie.

HERBIE: What if you have a tough word like Laurel? I keep getting the a and u mixed up, and I never remember which one comes first. The same thing happens with the o and u in pound.

OLIVIA: Oh! In that case you think of something like APES USE RADISHES for the a-u-r in Laurel, and OH UNI-CORN for the o-u in pound.

HERBIE: APES USE RADISHES! OH UNICORN! Why didn't I think of that? So *that's* how you make it on the Honor Roll!

OLIVIA: Funny, Erb.

HERBIE: You *are*, Olive.

NARRATOR: That week, Herbie carried his spelling list with him wherever he went. He practiced writing his words on paper, on frosty car windows, on his mother's meat-loaf—before it went in the oven—and in the gravel on the school playground. At 11:00 A.M. on Friday, Miss Pinkham passed out the white lined paper.

MISS PINKHAM: Put your name and date on the first highway.

NARRATOR: Miss Pinkham always referred to the blue lines on the paper as highways. When Annabelle Louisa Hodge-kiss finished writing her name and date neatly, she sat back in her chair.

ANNABELLE: I didn't even have to study—these words are a cinch.

HERBIE: (Talks to himself.) What a pain Annabelle can be! And she has the easiest street to spell too, Fish Street. Annabelle is in the highest reading group, the Wizards. They are *two* books ahead of us.

MISS PINKHAM: Boys and girls, those of you who want to try for the spelling bonus may do so now. Write your full name, address, town, state and zip code.

NARRATOR: Very carefully, Herbie printed his street address. When he came to his zip code, Herbie was in trouble.

HERBIE: 0 . . . 6 . . . 7 . . . 9 . . . What is that last number of my zip code?

MISS PINKHAM: Pass your papers in, please.

HERBIE: What *is* that number?

MISS PINKHAM: Herbie! You are keeping the entire class.

HERBIE: 0 . . . 6 . . . 7 . . . 9 . . . ?

MISS PINKHAM: Herbie Jones, if you don't hand me your paper by the time I count to three . . .

HERBIE: THREE! That's it!

NARRATOR: Annabelle raised her hand.

ANNABELLE: Miss Pinkham, I can't wait to get my postcard in the mail tomorrow. Can't you tell us *now* who got one hundred percent?

MISS PINKHAM: Looking through this mess of papers, I wonder if *anyone* got one hundred percent. There are so many careless errors!

NARRATOR: Saturday afternoon Herbie sat on his porch and waited. And watched . . . for the mail.

HERBIE: Is that him coming around the corner? It is! It's the mailman!

NARRATOR: Herbie raced into the house and grabbed a book off the coffee table. It was *Ten Days to Slimmer Thighs*. Mr. Jones, who had just shaved, walked toward the door. Herbie looked up and noticed he still had some soap around his ears.

HERBIE: Morning, Dad.

MR. JONES: Morning, Herbie. Nice to see you reading. Guess I better check on the mail. (Starts to groan.) Let's see, what's in this mess . . . Whistleman's Department Store, Occupant. HEY, HERBIE!

HERBIE: (Hopeful.) Yeah?

MR. JONES: You got a postcard. Your teacher said *you* were the *only* student to get a hundred percent on your spelling bonus.

HERBIE: YAHOO!

MR. JONES: That's the best news I've found in the mail in a long time. Come over here, spelling champ. Let's hug like bears.

HERBIE/MR. JONES: (They give wraparound hugs.)

NARRATOR: Monday morning right after the Pledge of Allegiance, Miss Pinkham asked . . .

MISS PINKHAM: Will the one person who received the ONLY postcard please rise?

NARRATOR: Everyone looked at Annabelle.

ANNABELLE: (Embarrassed.) I . . . I forgot to capitalize Connecticut.

ALL: *Who* got the postcard?

HERBIE: (Stands up and raises hand.) Me.

ALL: HERBIE JONES? But he's an Apple!

MISS PINKHAM: Herbie's paper Friday was outstanding. I think we should give him a big round of applause for his achievement.

ALL: (Clap.)

2

Annabelle's
Birthday Party

Characters: Narrator   Mrs. Hodgekiss
          Raymond Martin   Annabelle Louisa Hodgekiss
          Herbie Jones   Margie Sherman
          SFX Person   John Greenweed

Settings: School cafeteria; Annabelle's house

Time: A week in early March

NARRATOR: Herbie and Ray carried their lunch trays to an empty table in the school cafeteria and sat down.

RAYMOND: Look, Herbie! I got an invitation to Annabelle's birthday party . . . just like you did!

HERBIE: Yeah, I see it. I don't know what's so hot about going to Annabelle's dumb birthday party.

22

RAYMOND: She's a WIZARD and the smartest girl in the whole class. All the Wizards will be at her party.

HERBIE: So?

RAYMOND: So they're all teacher's pets. We go to this party, and bingo, we'll be teacher's pets too.

HERBIE: I doubt it, Ray. (Pauses.) Do you know what RSVP means?

RAYMOND: Hmmm . . . beats me. I'll go ask one of my sixth-grade friends. Just a minute.

NARRATOR: Herbie watched Ray go over to the sixth-grade table. When he returned, he sat down and slurped his milk.

SFX PERSON: SSSsssssluuuurp! Ssssluuurrrp!

RAYMOND: RSVP means remove shoes very promptly. She probably has a very neat house.

HERBIE: They told you that?

RAYMOND: Well, they said they considered me one of the guys, that's why they told me what it meant.

HERBIE: Yeah?

NARRATOR: Saturday afternoon, Herbie went to Annabelle's birthday party. Mrs. Hodgekiss answered the doorbell.

SFX PERSON: Bzzzzzzz. Bzzzzzzz.

MRS. HODGEKISS: Hello, Herbie. I'm glad you could come.

NARRATOR: Herbie took off his shoes and went into the living room. When he saw Ray, he went over and sat next to him on the couch.

HERBIE: We're the only ones with our shoes off.

RAYMOND: Guess we're the smartest guys here.

NARRATOR: Herbie looked at the coffee table.

HERBIE: What's this?

RAYMOND: Guacamole dip—smashed green stuff with lemon juice. You're supposed to put it on a potato chip. Try one.

SFX PERSON: (Makes eating noise.)

RAYMOND: I can't eat that green stuff myself. It reminds me of you know what. (Sniffs.)

NARRATOR: Suddenly, Herbie didn't feel like eating. He folded the leftover dip in a napkin and put it on the couch next to him. Then Annabelle came over.

ANNABELLE: Hi, Herbie.

HERBIE: Happy birthday, Annabelle.

ANNABELLE: This seat taken?

HERBIE: No.

SFX PERSON: CRUNCH. Squish.

HERBIE: Nice party.

MRS. HODGEKISS: Time to eat!

NARRATOR: Everyone stampeded to the dining room. Herbie followed Annabelle. She had a small green stain right *there*.

MRS. HODGEKISS: Dig in, kids!

NARRATOR: After everyone ate lunch, Mrs. Hodgekiss brought in the gifts.

ANNABELLE: Oh, Margie. What pretty stationery! Thank you.

NARRATOR: Annabelle opened John's present.

MARGIE: (Shrieks.) Look! It's a flowered T-shirt and panties!

ALL: (Laugh.)

ANNABELLE: I'll open Raymond's gift next. (Groans.) A purple pen . . . how nice . . . thank you.

NARRATOR: For some reason, Herbie's gift was last.

ANNABELLE: Gee, Herbie, it's heavy.

HERBIE: (To himself.) I hope Mom doesn't miss it from her cupboard.

NARRATOR: Everyone leaned forward to watch Annabelle unwrap the aluminum foil.

ANNABELLE: A can of pink salmon?

HERBIE: We've been studying Alaska in class. I thought you might like to have some food from there.

ANNABELLE: Hmmmmm, pink salmon . . .

RAYMOND: Why don't you open up the can? Let's see what's inside.

JOHN: There's a pink salmon in there, nerd-face.

RAYMOND: Maybe it's alive?

JOHN: Oh sure, Ray—that salmon is probably swimming around in that can right now. I hear something . . . it sounds like the ocean.

ANNABELLE: That's enough, John. Actually, I've never seen a pink salmon. Mom, would you get the can opener so we can look at it?

MRS. HODGEKISS: Now, dear?

ANNABELLE: Sure. How many want to see what pink salmon looks like?

ALL (But John): Me!

ANNABELLE: Majority wins. Mom, where's the can opener?

NARRATOR: After it was open, the smell of fish wafted through the dining room.

MARGIE: I'm holding my nose.

JOHN: Yuck!

ANNABELLE: Look at all the little black things and tiny bones in it.

NARRATOR: Annabelle passed the can around. When it came to Raymond, he turned green. And then Raymond launched it all over the tablecloth.

MARGIE: AAAAAUGH! Raymond BARFED!

MRS. HODGEKISS: I'll get some towels!

JOHN: There's yellow barf all over the carrot dish and yellow barf floating in Margie's water glass.

MARGIE: AAAAAAAAUGH!

HERBIE: Are you okay, Ray?

RAYMOND: I'm fine.

MRS. HODGEKISS: Sometimes these things just happen. Let's have some birthday cake now.

ALL: Eweyee look! The cake has yellow icing!

NARRATOR: No one had a piece of cake except Raymond.

RAYMOND: Can I have seconds?

ALL: (Groan.)

3

Haunted Bathrooms

Characters: Narrator   Mr. Bob
           Margie Sherman   Miss Pinkham
           Herbie Jones   Annabelle Louisa Hodgekiss
           Raymond Martin

Setting: School

Time: Morning

NARRATOR: Herbie and Raymond stood in the school hall-way waiting for the morning bell to ring. When they heard screaming in the basement, they dashed downstairs to see what was going on.

MARGIE: They're HAUNTED!

HERBIE: Huh?

RAYMOND: What is?

29

MARGIE: THE BATHROOMS!

NARRATOR: Herbie and Raymond peeked in the boys' bathroom. Mr. Bob was busy mopping up.

RAYMOND: What happened?

MR. BOB: The principal just asked me to clean up extra good this morning. He said some kids were passing rumors about the bathroom being haunted.

HERBIE/RAYMOND: Oh.

MR. BOB: If there are any ghosts around here, this Lysol and Clorox will get 'em.

NARRATOR: Ray stepped inside.

RAYMOND: Hey, Herb. Come here. Look what I see in the tall wastebasket . . . BONES!

HERBIE: BONES?

NARRATOR: Herbie walked inside and reached in the wastebasket.

HERBIE: (Holds bone up.) You mean this?

RAYMOND: Aaaauugh! I'm gettin' out of here. HERBIE FOUND HUMAN BONES!

NARRATOR: Miss Pinkham had a hard time getting the class to be quiet.

MISS PINKHAM: (Claps 3 times.) ENOUGH! I think, boys and girls, this bathroom business has gotten out of hand. Let's talk about it . . . one by one. Please raise your hands.

ANNABELLE: I . . . I . . . saw the word BL . . . BL . . . BL . . . BLOOD written in blood!

RAYMOND: Herbie found human bones in the wastepaper basket.

MISS PINKHAM: Do you have them?

HERBIE: One of them.

MISS PINKHAM: May I see it?

NARRATOR: Everyone watched Herbie walk up the aisle. Some kids moved away as he passed by. No one made a sound.

MARGIE: Ah . . . ah . . .ahchoo!

ALL: AAAHH! (Jump and fall back in their seats.)

MISS PINKHAM: Class, there is nothing to be afraid of. Herbie just handed me a chicken bone.

ALL: PHEW!

HERBIE: I thought so! That's the bone my sister and I pull on to make a wish.

MISS PINKHAM: I think this has gone entirely too far. Someone is playing a practical joke, and it's not funny. It's time to carry on with our day.

MARGIE: I'm not using the bathroom anymore.

RAYMOND: Me neither.

MISS PINKHAM: You mean to tell me NO ONE will use the bathrooms anymore?

ANNABELLE: I . . . I . . . need to.

MISS PINKHAM: Of course, Annabelle, you may go. We'll carry on as usual, now that using the bathrooms is no longer a big deal. It's time for a penmanship lesson.

NARRATOR: Five minutes later, Herbie walked quietly up to the teacher's desk.

HERBIE: (Whispering.) Ah . . . Miss Pinkham . . .

MISS PINKHAM: (Whispering.) Yes, Herbie.

HERBIE: Annabelle's not back yet from downstairs.

NARRATOR: Miss Pinkham turned white.

MISS PINKHAM: Oh, my goodness! (Whispering.) Will you go down and check on her? I don't want to bring the subject up again. The class has finally settled down.

HERBIE: Sure.

NARRATOR: When Herbie got halfway down the hall, he started talking to himself.

HERBIE: Check on Annabelle? That means going into the girls' bathroom. (Pause.) But . . . I *have* to do it. Miss Pinkham needs me.

NARRATOR: Herbie hurried down to the girls' bathroom. He was glad the door was propped open.

HERBIE: I'll just call her name. Ann . . . Annabelle?

NARRATOR: There was no answer.

HERBIE: ANNABELLE!

ANNABELLE: (In a soft voice.) I'm in here.

HERBIE: Are you okay?

ANNABELLE: I . . . can't move.

HERBIE: Huh?

ANNABELLE: I'm . . . too scared.

NARRATOR: Herbie peeked around the door. Annabelle was standing in one corner of the girls' bathroom, frozen stiff.

HERBIE: Just come on out. Miss Pinkham sent me to get you.

ANNABELLE: I . . . I can't move, Herbie. The bathroom ghost will get me!

HERBIE: Don't be silly. That's a big joke. Remember those bones? They were chicken bones. Just walk out.

ANNABELLE: It says THE GHOST IS HERE in blood.

HERBIE: That's probably red fingernail polish. It looks like the kind my sister uses. Come on out, Annabelle.

NARRATOR: When Herbie didn't hear anything, he said firmly,

HERBIE: I'M COMING IN!

NARRATOR: Herbie said it loud the way janitors do just in case someone is in there.

HERBIE: HERE I COME, ANNABELLE!

NARRATOR: Herbie stormed in the bathroom, grabbed Annabelle's arm and raced back into the hallway.

ANNABELLE: Herbie, weren't you afraid?

HERBIE: Of course I was. A boy's not supposed to be in the girls' bathroom.

4

The Murder

Characters: Narrator   Customer 2
Olivia Jones   Mrs. Jones
Herbie Jones   Mr. Pellizini
Customer 1   Policeman or Policewoman

Settings: Herbie's house; Dipping Donuts

Time: After school

NARRATOR: When Herbie got home from school, he heard his sister, Olivia, running the vacuum cleaner. He wasn't used to seeing his sister cleaning up.

OLIVIA: I can't believe how dirty this house is.

HERBIE: What's going on? Someone must be coming over.

OLIVIA: *Lance Pellizini* is coming over.

HERBIE: Who?

OLIVIA: The most popular boy at Laurel Woods Junior High.

HERBIE: Why would a guy like that want to see you?

OLIVIA: Get lost, Erb. We're going to study for a test in World History tomorrow.

HERBIE: Sure, Olive.

NARRATOR: Herbie walked into the bathroom. He had to go. He also wanted to tell Gus and Spike, his pet spiders, about his rotten day. When he got there he turned white.

HERBIE: OLIVIA, WHAT DID YOU DO?

OLIVIA: Geez, Erb. I just cleaned up in there. It was awful . . . including those two spiderwebs up in the corners of the ceiling.

HERBIE: YOU MURDERER! You murdered Gus and Spike. How could you!

NARRATOR: Herbie started pelting his sister with his fists.

OLIVIA: That hurts, you brat! I'm slapping you back.

HERBIE: (To himself.) Aha! The shampoo bottle is missing its cap. I'll just grab that and dump it on Olivia's hair. THAT'S what she thinks is most important—HER HAIR!

OLIVIA: STOP IT! STOP IT!

HERBIE: I'm dousing green stuff all over your hair!

OLIVIA: (Starts to cry.) It's dripping into my eyes and nose. (Sniffs.) Just wait till Mom gets home. I'M TELLING!

HERBIE: I'll NEVER forgive you, Olive. NEVER! EVER!

NARRATOR: Herbie ran out of the house and down to Dipping Donuts. His mother was pouring coffee when he stormed into the restaurant.

HERBIE: She KILLED them, Mom! She killed them!

CUSTOMERS 1/2: Ooooooooh!

MRS. JONES: Herbie! What are you talking about?

NARRATOR: Mrs. Jones came out from around the counter and held her son tight.

MRS. JONES: Calm down, dear.

NARRATOR: Mr. Pellizini dashed out of the back room waving his chef's hat in the air.

MR. PELLIZINI: What's going on? I was in the back cutting donuts.

CUSTOMER 1: *That boy* just saw a murder!

MR. PELLIZINI: A *murder?*

CUSTOMER 2: There's a policeman here. Why doesn't he investigate?

POLICEMAN: I *am* a police officer, young man. Tell me your story.

HERBIE: My sister, Olivia, she killed them in the bathroom with a broom, soap and the Clorox.

CUSTOMERS 1/2: The bathroom. Eweyeeeee. Clorox? Eweyeeeee.

POLICEMAN: Just a minute, I'm writing this down. "Murder weapons . . . broom and household chemicals." Hmm, very unusual . . .

HERBIE: She did it because of her friend.

POLICEMAN: Ahhhhhh . . . the motive. Do you know his name?

HERBIE: Ye . . . yes . . . Lance Pellizini.

MR. PELLIZINI: Lance Pellizini! Lance Pellizini is MY SON!

NARRATOR: A few of the customers sipped their coffee and munched on donuts as they continued catching every word of the conversation.

CUSTOMERS 1/2: (Sip coffee and munch on donuts.)

MR. PELLIZINI: My son! I don't believe it!

MRS. JONES: (Sighs with relief.) Olivia murdered Gus and Spike?

HERBIE: Ye . . . yes!

POLICEMAN: Deceased . . . Gus and Spike. (Pauses.) Who are they?

MRS. JONES: Gus and Spike are my son's pet spiders.

CUSTOMERS 1/2: (Chuckle. Sip coffee and munch.)

POLICEMAN: Easiest murder I ever solved.

MRS. JONES: I'm so sorry, Herbie. I know how important the spiders were to you. I should have told Olivia about them. I just didn't expect her to be cleaning up the house.

HERBIE: Mom . . . (Starts to cry.)

MRS. JONES: I know, dear. I feel bad too.

NARRATOR: When Herbie and his mother went home at five o'clock, Olivia was still rinsing the shampoo out of her hair.

OLIVIA: MOTHER! Do you *know* what Herbie did?

MRS. JONES: All right, dear, we'll talk about it.

NARRATOR: When Olivia found out that Mr. Pellizini was the manager of Dipping Donuts, she suddenly changed her mood.

OLIVIA: You work for him? *Lance Pellizini's* father?

MRS. JONES: Yes, why?

OLIVIA: Oh, Mother, really? (Sighs.) I know I wasn't happy about your new job at Dipping Donuts. (Groans.) You have to wear those dumb purple and white striped uniforms and purple caps. But now that I know you work for *Lance's* father, I'm *thrilled* about your job.

NARRATOR: Then Olivia looked at her brother.

OLIVIA: I'm *not* thrilled with you, Erb! I'll get even somehow. Maybe when you least expect it, I'll sneak up behind you and dump shampoo on *your* head!

HERBIE: Heh! Heh! Just try it!

MRS. JONES: Now, now, that's enough, you two!

5

Noontime Showdown

Characters: Narrator   Herbie Jones

             Raymond Martin   Margie Sherman

Settings: Classroom; cafeteria

Time: Late morning

NARRATOR: Monday morning, Ray sat at his desk moaning and groaning.

RAYMOND: You're lucky, Herbie. Miss Pinkham promoted *you* to the next highest reading group. (Groans.) There's no way I could *ever* get out of the Apples. I'm stuck for the rest of the year.

HERBIE: Wait a minute. I just got a sudden inspiration. I know how you can get out of the Apples reading group.

RAYMOND: How?

41

HERBIE: Just change the name to something else.

RAYMOND: YAHOO! (Pauses.) How do I do that?

HERBIE: Get Margie to go along with you and her two friends will too.

RAYMOND: Yeah?

HERBIE: What name would you like to have for your reading group?

RAYMOND: I don't want to be a piece of fruit again or something dumb like the Peppermint Patties. I'd like an exciting name, something different.

HERBIE: Hmmmmmmmm.

RAYMOND: Beavers? Nah! That's boring. Do you have any suggestions, Herbie? I just know what I *don't* want.

HERBIE: Well . . . I think insects are neat. You could be the Cockroaches, or Bloodsuckers, or . . . Spiders.

RAYMOND: That's PERFECT! I'd love to be the Spiders. Thanks, Herbie.

HERBIE: Okay, Ray, here's how you do it. Ask Margie to join us for lunch. Then be thinking about some good reasons why your group should change its name to Spiders.

RAYMOND: Ooooooh . . . I know one reason already. Spiders catch flies, squish their bodies and suck their blood. Neato, huh?

HERBIE: Ray, I think you should borrow my copy of *Charlotte's Web*. I'll show you where there are some good sentences that talk about spiders.

NARRATOR: At noontime, the boys went to the cafeteria. When Ray saw Margie, he was a little nervous about asking a girl to eat lunch with them.

RAYMOND: Come and j-j-j-join us, Margie.

NARRATOR: Margie set her tray of hot food down at the boys' table.

MARGIE: Thanks, Ray. I didn't know who I was going to eat with today. Isn't that awful that Annabelle got the chicken pox?

HERBIE/RAYMOND: (Trying not to smile.) Yeah.

NARRATOR: Ray thought he should ease into the conversation.

RAYMOND: Ever have the chicken pox, Margie?

MARGIE: Yes. Last spring. Did you guys?

NARRATOR: Both of them shook their heads no.

MARGIE: My mom said it's better to get them when you're young. Want my glazed pineapple ring? I hate it.

HERBIE: Nah.

RAYMOND: Thanks.

NARRATOR: Ray popped it whole in his mouth.

RAYMOND: By the way, Margie, I was thinking. Why don't we change our reading group name?

MARGIE: Would Miss Pinkham let us?

HERBIE: Sure! She told me we could change our names any-time everyone agreed.

MARGIE: Well, I loved our name, the Apples, but the apple season *is* over. Ha, ha!

NARRATOR: Raymond ha-hahed too, just to butter her up.

RAYMOND: Ha, ha, ha.

MARGIE: What do you think would be a good name, Ray?

NARRATOR: Ray wanted to make spiders sound good so he suggested something *really* gross first.

RAYMOND: I think BLOODSUCKERS would be terrific.

MARGIE: Aaaaaaaauuugh! You're kidding!

RAYMOND: No, it's different.

MARGIE: Well, I'm definitely not going to be a Bloodsucker. (Hits table with fist.)

NARRATOR: When Margie hit the table with her fist, a peach slice bounced out of her tray.

RAYMOND: Well, how 'bout Spiders then?

MARGIE: I don't know.

RAYMOND: Of course, we're not talking about ordinary spiders.

MARGIE: We're not?

RAYMOND: No. I'm talking about the spiders who are related to someone FAMOUS.

MARGIE: You are? Like who?

RAYMOND: Charlotte.

MARGIE: Charlotte?

RAYMOND: You want that peach slice?

MARGIE: No! It's dirty; it's been on the table.

RAYMOND: I'll take it.

NARRATOR: Ray leaned across with his fork, stabbed the peach and popped it in his mouth.

HERBIE: Aaaugh . . . gross!

RAYMOND: You know—*Charlotte's Web*.

MARGIE: Oh, you mean *that* Charlotte; she was really nice. Mom read me the story, and I saw the movie.

RAYMOND: I happen to have the sentence here that Charlotte said about spiders.

MARGIE: Really? Read it to me.

NARRATOR: Margie waited as Ray found his place and read from *Charlotte's Web*.

RAYMOND: Page thirty-seven: " 'Well, I *am* pretty,' " replied Charlotte." Page forty: " 'Nobody feeds me. . . . I have to be sharp and clever, lest I go hungry.' "

MARGIE: Hmmmmmmm, so spiders are sharp and clever?

RAYMOND: Yup.

MARGIE: And they're pretty?

RAYMOND: Very.

MARGIE: Looks aren't everything. What do spiders do?

HERBIE: It says right here on the next page. Spiders save the world from destruction. They help keep the bug population down.

MARGIE: Well . . . I guess we can call ourselves Spiders. I'll just have to bug the other two girls about it. Ha! Ha! But it shouldn't be too hard. They both love Charlotte.

RAYMOND: YAHOO!

NARRATOR: On the way home from school, Herbie put his arm around Raymond.

RAYMOND: We did it! We're no longer Apples. It's a great feeling!

HERBIE: This calls for a celebration. Let's go to my house for some day-old Dipping Donuts. When you crunch into those buggers you find out what tough is.

RAYMOND: Like us?

HERBIE: Like us.

Part Two

What's the Matter with
Herbie Jones?

The Ghost of Annabelle

Characters: Narrator   Mr. Hodgekiss
SFX Person   Annabelle Louisa Hodgekiss
Herbie Jones

Setting: Annabelle's house

Time: After school

NARRATOR: Herbie rang Annabelle's doorbell.

SFX PERSON: Bzzzzzzz. Bzzzzzz.

HERBIE: I wish I didn't have to deliver these get well cards from the class. But the teacher said I *had* to because I live the closest. (Groans.)

NARRATOR: Mr. Hodgekiss answered the door.

MR. HODGEKISS: Hello, Herbie.

HERBIE: Hello, Mr. Hodgekiss. My teacher wanted me to drop these cards by for Annabelle. Would you please give them to her? (Waves good-bye.) Thanks, bye.

NARRATOR: Herbie turned around and headed down the steps.

MR. HODGEKISS: Just a minute, Herbie. Won't you come in and give the cards to Annabelle yourself? The doctor said she isn't contagious anymore.

HERBIE: (To himself.) Whoa. I was supposed to deliver these cards to the door. Not go *in*. Miss Pinkham never said I had to do *that*.

MR. HODGEKISS: Just for a minute?

SFX PERSON: (Clears throat.)

HERBIE: Well . . . okay, Mr. Hodgekiss.

NARRATOR: Herbie felt his throat getting dry and raspy as he walked inside the house. When they got to Annabelle's door, they stopped.

MR. HODGEKISS: Before we go in, I must tell you something. Annabelle has been very stubborn about having the chicken pox.

SFX PERSON: (Clears throat again.)

HERBIE: (Answers like a squeaky frog.) Reaaaally?

NARRATOR: Herbie tried to act surprised but the fact was Herbie already knew Annabelle was stubborn—about everything.

MR. HODGEKISS: She insists on putting the sheet over her head every time someone comes in the room. She won't even let *me* see her face. Just her mother. She says when the spots and scabs are gone in a few days, she won't hide behind the sheet.

HERBIE: (To Mr. Hodgekiss.) No kidding? Annabelle has a sheet over her head? (To himself.) This is great! I didn't want to see her anyway.

MR. HODGEKISS: Maybe you'll have better luck. (Knocks on door.) May we come in, Annabelle?

ANNABELLE: Who's with you?

MR. HODGEKISS: Someone from school. He has some get well cards for you.

NARRATOR: Mr. Hodgekiss opened the door slowly. Herbie saw Annabelle sitting up in bed. The sheet was tucked behind her head.

ANNABELLE: Who is it?

MR. HODGEKISS: See for yourself, dear.

NARRATOR: Mr. Hodgekiss smiled as he walked out of the room. Herbie quickly looked around and sat down in a chair by Annabelle's desk.

SFX PERSON: (Coughs a few times and then clears throat.)

HERBIE: Hi . . . hi . . . Annabelle.

ANNABELLE: Do you have a cold, John, or is that your asthma acting up again?

HERBIE: (To himself.) John? Hey, this could be fun. I'm visiting a ghost and now I can even pretend to be someone else. (To Annabelle.) Just . . . just my asthma.

ANNABELLE: Did you bring me some cards?

HERBIE: Yup. Here's two.

ANNABELLE: Read them to me.

HERBIE: Sure. Here's one with a Viking ship on it.

ANNABELLE: I know that's from Raymond Martin. He always draws Viking ships.

HERBIE: Yup, and on the inside it says, "Bon Voyage."

ANNABELLE: BON VOYAGE? That's dumb. Bon Voyage means have a good trip. Having the chicken pox is NOT having fun, and you certainly can't go anywhere.

NARRATOR: Herbie remembered to cough a few times and act like John.

SFX PERSON: (Coughs, wheezes and sneezes.)

HERBIE: Here's a real nice card. It has you in bed with your cat and a thermometer in your mouth.

ANNABELLE: Hmmmmm, I wonder who made that one?

HERBIE: It even has a poem inside. I'll read it.

> Annabelle, Annabelle
> Sick in bed
> Spots on her nose
> And spots on her head
> Think I will give her a
> Bright red rose
> Then she knows
> I will tickle her toes
> With it.

ANNABELLE: (Giggles.) That's funny! Who wrote it?

NARRATOR: Herbie tipped back his chair.

HERBIE: Herbie Jones.

ANNABELLE: Herbie Jones wrote *that*?

HERBIE: The one and only.

NARRATOR: Annabelle was quiet for a moment.

ANNABELLE: Well, you know, John . . .

HERBIE: Yes, Annabelle . . .

ANNABELLE: I'm not speaking to Herbie . . .

HERBIE: Oh?

NARRATOR: Herbie leaned forward and listened. He was curious why Annabelle had put three red checks after his name on her notepad at school.

ANNABELLE: Herbie Jones wore earrings to school in October. It was Halloween, and he was supposed to be a pirate. Everyone knows a pirate wears just one *gold* earring. Herbie wore a pair of strawberries.

HERBIE: (To himself.) That's check one.

ANNABELLE: . . . and when he wrote a story at Thanksgiving about a turkey who got his head chopped off, he called the turkey Annabelle.

HERBIE: (Trying not to laugh. Holds up two fingers for victory.)

ANNABELLE: (Groans.) . . . *and* he gave me a can of *salmon* for my birthday.

HERBIE: (To himself.) Check three. What a memory she has.

I better get out of here. It's getting dangerous. I've played John long enough. I'll sneeze once and then head for the door.

SFX PERSON: (Sneezes once loudly.)

ANNABELLE: But . . . Herbie Jones does have a way with words.

NARRATOR: Herbie stopped at the door.

HERBIE: Herbie Jones has a way with words?

ANNABELLE: IF YOU TELL HERBIE I SAID THAT, JOHN GREENWEED, I'LL KILL YOU!

NARRATOR: Herbie snatched a Kleenex from the flowered box on Annabelle's desk and held it up to his mouth. This was no time to be discovered.

HERBIE: I won't. Your secret is safe with me. (Removes Kleenex and smiles.)

NARRATOR: Mr. Hodgekiss saw Herbie to the door.

MR. HODGEKISS: Did she talk to you face to face?

HERBIE: (Feeling guilty.) No. She even thinks . . . I'm . . . John Greenweed. I kind of went along with it.

MR. HODGEKISS: Listen, Herbie, if my daughter wants to play games, you can too. Your secret is safe with me . . . John.

HERBIE: Thanks, Mr. Hodgekiss!

NARRATOR: As Herbie shuffled along the sidewalk, he kept thinking about what Annabelle had said. Herbie Jones has a way with words.

HERBIE: Is that really true? Maybe I should try making up a few more poems. Let's see . . .

>   Spaghetti is red
>   Meatballs are brown
>   You make them with eggs
>   And a pound of ground round.

>   When the sun is yellow
>   It's time to play.
>   When the sun is red,
>   It's time to go to bed.

(Clicks fingers.) I do have a way with words!

2

The Dance Contest

Characters: Narrator   Herbie Jones
Miss Pinkham   Annabelle Louisa Hodgekiss
Mrs. Coffey   John Greenweed
Raymond Martin   Cowboy (on the record)

Setting: School gym

Time: Afternoon

NARRATOR: At one-thirty, Miss Pinkham led the class briskly down to the gym in two straight, quiet lines. She had the girls stand on one side of the gym and the boys on the other.

MISS PINKHAM: Today we have our first dance contest. Our thanks go to Margie Sherman for making the paper trophies . . .

CLASS: (Claps.)

MISS PINKHAM: . . . and to all of you for learning the dance steps so well this year. I've asked our cook, Mrs. Coffey, to sit in and do the judging. Thank you, Mrs. Coffey.

CLASS: (Claps.)

MRS. COFFEY: It's nice to get out of the kitchen for a break!

RAYMOND: (Whispers to Herbie.) Our foolproof plan for getting out of this dance contest is working perfectly! All we have to do is walk like snails across the gym floor, and when we get to the other side . . .

HERBIE: . . . all the girls will be chosen. We'll have no partners because there are two more boys in class today.

RAYMOND/HERBIE: Yeah! (They slap each other five.)

MISS PINKHAM: Now, get ready for a boys' choice.

ANNABELLE: Miss Pinkham?

MISS PINKHAM: Yes, Annabelle, I was just going to put the needle on the record. What is it?

ANNABELLE: Every time we have dancing, we have a boys' choice. Can't we have a girls' choice for a change?

RAYMOND/HERBIE: Oh, no!

MISS PINKHAM: That's a splendid idea. I should have thought of it myself. Routine can do that to a teacher.

MRS. COFFEY: That's why I try to vary my menus.

MISS PINKHAM: Let's have a girls' choice. Our first number is a square dance.

HERBIE: I feel sick.

RAYMOND: I'm tying my shoes.

JOHN: I'm getting an asthma attack. (Starts to wheeze.)

HERBIE: Look at those girls running across the floor. They look like the U.S. cavalry. All they have to do is shout, "CHARGE!"

NARRATOR: Annabelle and Margie were the first two girls to make it across the gym floor.

ANNABELLE: John, shall we dance?

JOHN: (Wheezes and coughs a lot.)

ANNABELLE: You sound like you did when you stopped by my house a few days ago . . .

JOHN: Huh? (Coughs some more.)

NARRATOR: Herbie looked over. He was in trouble now. It was Herbie who stopped by Annabelle's house, *not* John. He just pretended he was John. Now Herbie had to act fast before Annabelle found out. Quickly, Herbie stepped in front of Annabelle.

HERBIE: Let's dance, Annabelle. John, you should see the nurse.

ANNABELLE: Herbie Jones, what are you doing?

NARRATOR: Herbie knew he had to do some fast talking. He was just glad no one was close enough to hear him.

HERBIE: Annabelle, you look so pretty in that yellow dress, I just HAVE to dance with you!

NARRATOR: Annabelle was quiet for a moment.

ANNABELLE: This is *supposed* to be a girl-ask-boy, and I was *supposed* to dance with John. John is the best dancer in our class. I don't want to be stuck with you in a dance contest. You *hate* to dance.

HERBIE: Me? Hate dancing? You're dead wrong.

ANNABELLE: I am?

HERBIE: (Lowers voice.) I've had dance lessons.

ANNABELLE: Dance lessons?

HERBIE: Yeah, my mom put me in a . . . a ballet class.

ANNABELLE: When?

HERBIE: When I was three.

ANNABELLE: Funny. Listen, Herbie, you better dance your very best because I want to win this contest.

HERBIE: Annabelle, you haven't seen anything yet.

NARRATOR: Miss Pinkham put on the record player. A cowboy started singing the words to a square dance.

COWBOY: (Claps four times.) YAHOO! YEEHAW! Welcome to the barn. We got a mighty fine dance for you. Guys, pick a perdy gal and take a bow. Gals, curtsey back.

HERBIE: Come on, Annabelle . . . curtsey. I'm takin' a bow.

ANNABELLE: All right, Herbie Jones, but you better dance your best.

COWBOY: (Claps four times.) Do-si-do your partner! Swing that perdy gal. YEEHAW!

HERBIE: Take my right hand and twirl underneath, Annabelle.

ANNABELLE: Oooooh! I'm spinning round and round! *Where* did you learn that step?

HERBIE: I saw two ice skaters do it on TV.

COWBOY: Down the center, Virginia reel! Clap and shout Yahoo!

HERBIE: It's our turn, Annabelle. Let's shake a leg!

ANNABELLE: Yahoo! We're flying!

HERBIE: YEEHAW! This is kind of fun.

MISS PINKHAM: (Claps.) Wonderful! Now, our next dance is a slow record. Remember the box step?

ALL: (Groan.)

MISS PINKHAM: Okay, take your positions.

NARRATOR: When Herbie put his arm on Annabelle's waist, he was close enough to smell her hair.

HERBIE: (Takes a deep sniff.) Mmmmmmmm! Your hair smells like our garbage can.

ANNABELLE: Garbage can! Herbie Jones, that's an insult!

HERBIE: No it isn't. There's a gardenia bush right next to it. That's why our garbage can smells so good.

ANNABELLE: Well . . . in that case . . . thank you.

HERBIE: Okay, Annabelle, let's do the box step.

ANNABELLE/HERBIE (together): Side-together-forward *AND* side-together-back. Side-together-forward *AND* side-together-back.

ANNABELLE: Why, Herbie, I didn't realize you were so good at this.

HERBIE: Hey, I was born with dancing shoes on.

ANNABELLE: (Laughs.)

NARRATOR: When the record was over, Herbie Jones was never the same again. He just kept staring at Annabelle as she waited to hear the results of their dance contest.

MRS. COFFEY: The winners are . . . Herbie Jones and Annabelle Louisa Hodgekiss.

ANNABELLE: We won, Herbie! We won!

CLASS: (Claps.)

NARRATOR: Raymond shook his head on the way home from school.

RAYMOND: Well, Herbie, our foolproof plan sure backfired. I had to dance with Margie Sherman and you . . . you had to dance with Annabelle Louisa Hodgekiss. Feel sick?

HERBIE: (In a trance.) Hmmmm.

RAYMOND: Yo, Herbie! (Clicks fingers.) Are you there?

HERBIE: Huh?

RAYMOND: Feel sick from dancing with a girl?

HERBIE: No. It was kind of . . . fun.

RAYMOND: Fun? Are you all right, Herbie?

HERBIE: I'm fine.

RAYMOND: Good. Let's go to my house for some fizzy lemonade.

HERBIE: Sorry, Ray, I can't. Annabelle asked me to go to her house and write a few poems.

RAYMOND: She did?

HERBIE: (Nods.) Uh-huh.

RAYMOND: And you're *going*?

HERBIE: Uh-huh. Annabelle says I have a way with words.

NARRATOR: Raymond watched his buddy turn up Fish Street.

RAYMOND: Wanting to spend the afternoon writing poems is bad enough, but (slaps side of his face) getting mixed up with a girl like Annabelle is trouble. I better keep a close eye on Herbie.

3

Under the
Library Table

Characters: Mrs. Jones   Herbie Jones
            Mr. Jones   SFX Person
            Olivia Jones   Annabelle Louisa Hodgekiss
            Narrator   Raymond Martin

Settings: Herbie's house; library

Time: Evening

Props: Some keys

MRS. JONES: HERBIE! Your dinner's getting cold.

MR. JONES: What's gotten into that boy? He's never late to dinner. Who wants some meatloaf?

OLIVIA: I do. Please.

NARRATOR: A few minutes later, Herbie sat down at the table.

HERBIE: Sorry, Mom. I had to brush my teeth.

MR. JONES: You brush *before* meals now?

OLIVIA: He wants his breath to smell nice for Annabelle. Did you have fun at her house today? Hmmmm?

NARRATOR: Herbie blew some breath in Olivia's face.

SFX PERSON: (Exhales loudly.)

OLIVIA: Hmmmm, wintergreen. Nice, Erb. I also like the way you combed your hair.

HERBIE: Thanks, *Olive!*

MR. JONES: Are you going somewhere tonight, son?

HERBIE: To the library.

OLIVIA: What are you studying at the library?

HERBIE: Poetry. Miss Pinkham told us we could make a book of poems together.

MRS. JONES: Miss Pinkham told who?

HERBIE: Annabelle and me.

OLIVIA: Hmmm. You might look up Carl Sandburg. He wrote a neat poem called "Fog." We read it in English last week.

HERBIE: Thanks, Olive. Carl who?

OLIVIA: Sandburg. It rhymes with Hamburg.

HERBIE: Got it! I told Annabelle I'd pick her up at six o'clock so I better get going.

NARRATOR: Twenty minutes later, Herbie and Annabelle walked up the steps to the library.

SFX PERSON: (Jingles some keys.)

ANNABELLE: What is that tinkling noise behind us? (Groans.) Oh, it's Raymond Martin and his dog, Shadow. I bet they're *following us*. Let's hurry up and go inside.

NARRATOR: Herbie and Annabelle dashed into the library and went over to the card catalogue.

ANNABELLE: Now, what poet did you want to look up, Herbie?

HERBIE: Uh . . . Carl Hamburger.

ANNABELLE: (Giggling.) I think you mean Carl Sandburg.

NARRATOR: Ray hurriedly tied Shadow to a parking meter in front of the library. Then he joined Herbie and Annabelle at the card catalogue.

RAYMOND: What'cha looking up?

HERBIE: Hi, Ray!

ANNABELLE: We're busy, Raymond.

HERBIE: Olivia told me some guy named Carl Sandburg writes good poetry. I want to read his poem "Fog." Here it is!

ANNABELLE: Shhhh! Let's read it over here. I'll put our other poetry books down on the table.

NARRATOR: Just as Raymond was about to sit down, Annabelle flared her nostrils.

SFX PERSON: (Inhales deeply and sniffs.)

ANNABELLE: Sorry, Raymond. There's *just* enough room for Herbie and me and our books. You can sit behind us at the next table. Read the poem, Herbie.

HERBIE: "Fog," by Carl Sandburg.

The fog comes
on little cat feet.

It sits looking
over harbor and city
on silent haunches
and then, moves on.

Gee, it doesn't rhyme!

NARRATOR: Raymond leaned over.

RAYMOND: It must not be a real poem.

HERBIE: No . . . it has to be a poem. Olivia said Carl Hamburger is a poet.

ANNABELLE: I like poems that rhyme better.

HERBIE: What does *haunches* mean?

ANNABELLE: I'll get the big Webster's dictionary, and we can look it up.

NARRATOR: When she returned, they flipped through the pages until they came to the H section.

ANNABELLE: Here it is. It says the two rounded parts of your lower back.

HERBIE: Rounded parts?

RAYMOND: They mean rear end.

ANNABELLE: (Giggles.) My mom always told me to call it derriere—that's the French word for it.

HERBIE: Derriere? We call them buns at my house.

HERBIE/ANNABELLE/RAYMOND: (Together they crack up.)

ANNABELLE: Shhhh! We're going to get in trouble. Wait a minute! What's that under the card catalogue? It has . . . four legs and it's . . . black and hairy.

HERBIE: Shadow!

RAYMOND: Where?

ANNABELLE: Over by the card catalogue. He's squatting.

RAYMOND: Oh, no! When he sits on his . . .

HERBIE: Haunches . . .

RAYMOND: That means he has to . . .

NARRATOR: Raymond dashed for his dog and pulled him outside.

SFX PERSON: (Makes running footsteps and barks three times.)

NARRATOR: While Shadow ran to a big bush, Raymond looked back through the glass door of the library at Herbie and Annabelle.

RAYMOND: Just look at them! They're still laughing about that dumb word, haunches. Herbie doesn't even care that I'm gone. They sure don't need me. What's the matter with Herbie anyway? Is he sick or something?

NARRATOR: Ray continued looking through the glass door. When Herbie's green notebook fell to the floor, Herbie and Annabelle crawled underneath the table.

HERBIE: Where did my notebook go?

ANNABELLE: I'll get it.

HERBIE: *I'll* get it.

HERBIE/ANNABELLE: Ouch! We bumped heads!

NARRATOR: Ray got up slowly.

RAYMOND: Oh, no. Herbie is staring into Annabelle's eyes and not moving. I know what's wrong with Herbie. He's sick all right. Lovesick. He likes a girl. He has the G Disease! I can't desert my buddy now! I'm keeping a close watch on things. Maybe there's time to save Herbie before it's too late.

4

It All Happened at the Fish Grotto

Characters: Narrator   Mr. Hodgekiss
         Herbie Jones   Annabelle Louisa Hodgekiss
         Mrs. Hodgekiss   SFX Person
         Waitress

Settings: Library; restaurant

Time: Saturday noon

NARRATOR: Saturday morning, Herbie and Annabelle worked on a poetry project at the library. At noon, Mr. and Mrs. Hodgekiss picked them up in the car and took them to lunch. Ray spied on them from the bushes.

HERBIE: Hey! We just passed Burger Paradise.

MRS. HODGEKISS: We're going to the Fish Grotto.

74

HERBIE: The Fish Grotto? That's a rich place. (Whispers.) I wonder if I brought enough pennies.

NARRATOR: Herbie had emptied his baseball bank and stuffed 261 pennies in his jeans pockets. He tried not to rattle as he walked into the restaurant lobby with Annabelle and her parents. A waitress greeted them.

WAITRESS: How many are in your party?

HERBIE: (To himself.) Party? We're not even wearing funny hats.

MR. HODGEKISS: Four, please.

WAITRESS: Thank you. If you'll follow me, I have a nice table by the picture of a sea captain. Please make yourselves comfortable and here are your menus.

NARRATOR: The Hodgekisses and Herbie studied their menus.

ANNABELLE: Hmmmmm, I'll have the Catch of the Day. Halibut.

MRS. HODGEKISS: Me too.

MR. HODGEKISS: How about you, Herbie?

HERBIE: Eh . . . eh . . . (To himself.) Gee, there's nothing on this menu for two dollars.

MR. HODGEKISS: I'm treating, you know.

HERBIE: You are? Well, then I'll have that hamburger and french fries plate.

ANNABELLE: Herbie, you DON'T order hamburger at a fish restaurant.

HERBIE: How come it's on the menu then?

ANNABELLE: Look where it is.

SFX PERSON: (GULPS loudly.)

NARRATOR: It was under the Kiddy Specials.

ANNABELLE: Why don't you just order what we are, the Catch of the Day?

HERBIE: Okay, I'll have the habit too.

ANNABELLE: Halibut!

HERBIE: (To himself.) She's beginning to sound like my sister.

NARRATOR: When the waitress returned with four hot plates, everyone sniffed the delicious fish aroma.

ALL: (Inhale deeply and sniff.) Ahhh!

WAITRESS: I hope you enjoy your meals.

MRS. HODGEKISS: Thank you. The food and service are always excellent here at the Grotto.

ANNABELLE: Herbie, use your napkin.

HERBIE: Okay! I'm putting it on my lap. See?

MRS. HODGEKISS: Lemon?

HERBIE: Thank you, Mrs. Hodgekiss. I like it on my fish.

NARRATOR: When Herbie squeezed the lemon, it slipped out of his hands and went flying into the picture of the sea captain hanging on the wall.

SFX PERSON: (Whistles, up high, then slaps three fingers on a hand for the lemon splat on the floor.)

HERBIE: Whooops! Oh, gee!

MR. HODGEKISS: That's okay, Herbie. The poor guy spends all his time up there watching all this food. Now he finally gets to taste some.

HERBIE: (Laughs.) Right. Well, I think I'll try this delicious fish.

NARRATOR: Just as Herbie cut into it with his fork, he saw something.

HERBIE: Hmmmm, what's this? A hair.

NARRATOR: Herbie tried to pull it out with his fingers but when he did, the fish dangled back and forth on the hair like a yo-yo.

SFX PERSON: (Makes whistling sound going up and then down.)

HERBIE: This is a job for my trusty tweezers.

NARRATOR: Herbie took them out of his back pocket and began the operation.

HERBIE: First I'll take the fork in my left hand and hold the fish still. Now I'll use my right hand to tweeze the hair out of the crust real eeeeeeasy.

SFX PERSON: (Makes a long kissing sound and then pops cheek once.)

HERBIE: Got it! How about that? It's a white one!

ANNABELLE: Blaaaaaugh! I'm NEVER eating here again as long as I live.

MRS. HODGEKISS: Eweyee! A nasty, despicable hair!

MR. HODGEKISS: I'll take care of this. *I'm* going to speak with the manager. I didn't know hair was on the menu.

MRS. HODGEKISS: Good! We'll meet you in the lobby, dear.

NARRATOR: Herbie followed Annabelle and her mother. When they got to the wishing well in the lobby, Annabelle stopped.

SFX PERSON: Clinkity, clink. Clinkity, clink.

ANNABELLE: What is making all that noise?

HERBIE: Oh, that's just the pennies in my pockets.

ANNABELLE: Pennies? Why, Herbie Jones, you wanted to treat me to some wishes all along. How many pennies did you bring?

HERBIE: Uh . . . two hundred or so.

ANNABELLE: Oh, Herbie! What a wonderful surprise! I'll start wishing just as soon as you put them in.

HERBIE: Them?

NARRATOR: Herbie dropped four pennies into the water.

SFX PERSON: Plunk! Plunk! Plunk! Plunk!

ANNABELLE: All of them!

HERBIE: All of them? This money was supposed to be for worms. Good-bye, worms. Hello, Annabelle. I sure don't think much of the trade.

5

To Cheat or Not To Cheat

Characters: Narrator   Phillip McDoogle
              Raymond Martin   Annabelle Louisa Hodgekiss
              John Greenweed   Miss Pinkham
              Herbie Jones

Settings: Cafeteria; John's house; Raymond's house; school

Time: Thursday, Friday

NARRATOR: Herbie and Ray carried their trays through the cafeteria lunch line.

RAYMOND: (Sniffs deeply.) Mmmmmmm . . . spaghetti!

JOHN: Hey, Herbie! Raymond! Come over here. We got two seats saved.

80

HERBIE: Thanks. I don't want to sit near Annabelle. She thinks I'm her boyfriend.

BOYS: Ooooooooh!

NARRATOR: Herbie remembered what his dad said about being straightforward and honest.

HERBIE: Look, she's not my girlfriend anymore. Okay? I just liked her for a day and a half. That's shorter than the chicken pox.

RAYMOND: Yeah, Herbie, but your G Disease was deadlier.

JOHN/PHILLIP: (Laugh.)

HERBIE: Ray's right. It was deadly. I found out how bossy Annabelle can be when we worked on our poetry project together. She kept telling me to write poems that rhyme when I didn't feel like it.

PHILLIP: I heard you guys went out to lunch. Where did you go?

HERBIE: To the Fish Grotto. That was deadly too. Annabelle told me what to order, how to use my napkin, and made me spend all my pennies on *her* at the wishing well.

RAYMOND: That money was supposed to be for worms.

BOYS: (Groan.)

HERBIE: I thought if I told her I had some girlfriend at another school, she'd get mad and not like me anymore. But it backfired. Annabelle says she loves a challenge. Now she likes me more.

BOYS: (Groan.)

JOHN: Who did you say your girlfriend was?

HERBIE: Someone named Pepper.

JOHN: Pepper who?

HERBIE: Pepper Roni.

BOYS: (Crack up.)

JOHN: Okay, you guys. Enough. Let's get to the meat of this conversation.

RAYMOND: Yeah, I'm popping this meatball right in my mouth.

JOHN: Not food, Ray. A *discovery*. The discovery of the century. Tell 'em about it, Phil.

PHILLIP: You guys know tomorrow is the spelling bee between the girls and the boys.

HERBIE/RAYMOND: Oh yeah!

JOHN: You didn't forget how the girls creamed us the last time? We *must* get revenge.

NARRATOR: Ray wiped some tomato sauce off his mouth with his sleeve.

PHILLIP: So, the good news is that I have found the word list for the spelling bee.

HERBIE/RAYMOND: YOU WHAT?

PHILLIP: (Lowering his voice.) Right next to Miss Pinkham's red porcupine pencil holder. I saw it when I walked by her desk this morning.

JOHN: All we have to do is go up to the teacher's desk and look at the words.

HERBIE: But that's *cheating*.

PHILLIP: So? Our honor is at stake, boys. If we lose another spelling bee to the girls, we're doomed.

HERBIE: You're going to cheat for honor?

PHILLIP: Yes.

RAYMOND: I was the first person to sit down in the last bee. I misspelled a tricky word.

JOHN: I remember that. You couldn't spell *is*.

PHILLIP/JOHN: (Laugh.)

RAYMOND: Funny, but I'll tell you something. *Is* sounds like i-z. There should be a z at the end, not an s.

JOHN: The question is, are we going to cheat or not?

PHILLIP: Cheat!

RAYMOND: Sounds fine to me. I'm tired of being the first one to sit down.

JOHN: I'm in. It's up to you, Herbie.

HERBIE: I think we should try to beat the girls fair and square.

JOHN: Sure, sure, Herbie, and *who* is going to spell better than Annabelle? She can spell *anything*.

HERBIE: So can I. A-n-y-t-h-i-n-g.

JOHN: Funny. You know what I mean. Annabelle wins everything.

NARRATOR: When Phillip said that, Raymond had a powerful idea.

RAYMOND: Just a minute, guys, I gotta have a word with Herbie.

NARRATOR: Ray pulled Herbie over to the drinking fountain.

RAYMOND: Look, Herbie, this is the perfect way to get out of your girlfriend mess. If we win the spelling bee, Annabelle will hate the boys for beating her. That includes you! We'll all get the silent treatment.

HERBIE: It would make things a lot easier. But it isn't right.

ANNABELLE: (Waves.) Yoohoo! Herbie!

HERBIE: Oh no.

RAYMOND: What's the matter?

HERBIE: Annabelle just winked at me. That's it! Count me in.

NARRATOR: The boys met at John's house right after school.

JOHN: Okay, guys, first things first. Pass the cheese balls. (Pauses.) Now, let's compare words.

RAYMOND: When I went up to the teacher's desk, I saw four words: pen, light, bulb, flour . . .

JOHN: Which flour? The kind you put in a vase or on chicken?

RAYMOND: (Pauses.) The kind you put in a vase: f-l-o-u-r.

NARRATOR: John wrote it down neatly on his portable blackboard.

PHILLIP: I copied down produce, coffee, sugar, and I think, cremate.

JOHN: My great-grandmother was cremated.

PHILLIP: So were we in the last spelling bee by the girls.

BOYS: (All groan.)

JOHN: Unusual word—cremate.

PHILLIP: How about the next one: cat litter. Who would think *that* would be on a spelling list.

RAYMOND: Tricky.

NARRATOR: The session continued for twenty minutes. Herbie remained quiet for most of the time. He just felt uncomfortable.

NARRATOR: At midnight that night, Raymond's phone rang.

RAYMOND: (In a sleepy voice.) Hello?

NARRATOR: Herbie decided to use their secret code.

HERBIE: 992, this is Double 030.

RAYMOND: Why are you calling so late?

HERBIE: We can't go through with that spelling bee tomorrow. It's not right, Raymond. We could get in a lot of trouble.

RAYMOND: No one is going to find out. Besides, you said yourself, it's the best way for you to stop this girlfriend stuff.

HERBIE: I have a better plan.

RAYMOND: What?

HERBIE: Let's take on the girls fair and square. I think we have a good chance.

RAYMOND: You're a dreamer, Herbie. And speaking of dreams, I was having a good one. Good night.

HERBIE: Just a minute, Ray!

RAYMOND: What?

HERBIE: What if your mom found out about our cheating?

RAYMOND: (Pauses.) She'd use that old Ping-Pong paddle with the rubber off one side.

HERBIE: Yeah, and you know which side she'd use on your . . . haunches!

NARRATOR: Ray smiled even though he was sleepy. He liked that word too.

RAYMOND: I'll think about it.

NARRATOR: The next morning the boys met at the maple treé.

PHILLIP: I think we're throwing a perfectly good plan down a rat hole.

JOHN: Yeah, we'll be washing the blackboard all week, and we'll get stomped today in the spelling bee.

HERBIE: We gotta do this, guys.

NARRATOR: The boys followed Herbie into the classroom and listened to his confession to Miss Pinkham.

MISS PINKHAM: Well, boys, that so-called spelling list wouldn't have helped you at all.

PHILLIP: It wouldn't have?

MISS PINKHAM: No. It was my grocery list.

BOYS: GROCERY LIST!

JOHN: But you had cremate on that list, Miss Pinkham. How could that be?

MISS PINKHAM: Cremate? Hmmm. (Laughs.) That was Cremora. I use it in my coffee.

JOHN: Oh!

MISS PINKHAM: You certainly did the right thing to tell me about it, boys. There will be no punishment.

JOHN: No punishment?

MISS PINKHAM: No.

JOHN: We have Herbie to thank for that, Miss Pinkham. It was his idea to tell you.

NARRATOR: Miss Pinkham patted Herbie on the back. Then the entire class applauded. Especially Annabelle.

HERBIE: (Whispers.) Oh no. Now she thinks I'm some kind of hero. She'll never give up on this girlfriend business. Unless . . . unless the boys pull off a miracle and win the spelling bee.

6

The Spelling Bee

Characters: Miss Pinkham   Sarah Sitwellington
Herbie Jones   Margie Sherman
Phillip McDoogle   Raymond Martin
John Greenwood   Narrator
Annabelle Louisa Hodgekiss

Setting: School classroom

Time: Morning

Prop: Bell

MISS PINKHAM: (Claps her hands twice.) Class, when I ring this bell, we will begin our spelling bee. Girls, I would like you to line up quietly by the windows. Boys, stand by the blackboard.

HERBIE: (To boys.) We gotta give this spelling bee our best shot, guys. I think we can do it. We have to.

90

BOYS: Yeah!

PHILLIP: (Holds fist up.) REVENGE!

BOYS: Yeah!

JOHN: The girls creamed us in the last spelling bee. This time, we *have* to win!

ANNABELLE: (To girls.) Okay, girls, we must do our best. We're the champs, right?

GIRLS: RIGHT!

ANNABELLE: *We'll* beat the boys again.

SARAH: Look who's up first for them—Raymond Martin. He'll miss!

MARGIE: Remember the last spelling bee? Raymond couldn't spell *is*.

MISS PINKHAM: (Rings bell.) Now . . . there is no talking. And, you MUST spell the word correctly the first time. Raymond, since you are at the front of the boys' line, you will go first.

GIRLS: (Few giggles.)

MISS PINKHAM: Raymond, spell . . . hamburger.

RAYMOND: I've seen that word lots of times at Burger Paradise! Mmmmm, hamburger. H-a-m-b-u-r-g-e-r.

MISS PINKHAM: Correct.

BOYS: (Cheer and clap.)

MISS PINKHAM: Shhhhhh! There will be no cheering during the spelling bee.

RAYMOND: Do you want me to spell fries or shake?

MISS PINKHAM: No, Raymond. I give the words. Not you. Margie, your word is germ.

MARGIE: (Steps forward.) Germ. J-e-r-m.

MISS PINKHAM: I'm sorry, that's incorrect. You'll have to sit down.

GIRLS: (Groan.)

NARRATOR: After Phillip spelled *germ* correctly, the boys wanted to clap, but they didn't dare. It was especially hard for Raymond to keep quiet. This was the first time he made it to round two in a spelling bee. The boys did a silent cheer instead. When it was Herbie's turn, it was pin-quiet.

MISS PINKHAM: Herbie Jones, spell pound.

HERBIE: I know that word. I got it right before on a spelling test. Pound. P-o-u-n-d.

MISS PINKHAM: Correct.

BOYS: (Thumbs up.)

MISS PINKHAM: Annabelle Louisa Hodgekiss.

ANNABELLE: (Steps forward and fluffs hair.) Yes?

MISS PINKHAM: Spell square.

ANNABELLE: Square. S-q-u-a-r-e.

MISS PINKHAM: Correct.

ANNABELLE: (Fluffs hair.) That word was a cinch.

MISS PINKHAM: John Greenweed, spell locomotive.

JOHN: Locomotive. L-o-c-o-m-o-t-i-v-e.

MISS PINKHAM: Correct.

BOYS: (Wave hands in the air.)

NARRATOR: The spelling bee continued back and forth for ten minutes.

MISS PINKHAM: Raymond, spell said.

RAYMOND: Ooooh, this is a tricky word. Said. S-e-d.

MISS PINKHAM: I'm sorry, you'll have to sit down.

BOYS: (Groan.)

GIRLS: (Wave hands in the air.)

NARRATOR: Most of the children were out by the fifth round.

MISS PINKHAM: Phillip, spell tweezers.

PHILLIP: Tweezers. T-w-e-z-e-r-s.

MISS PINKHAM: I'm sorry, that's incorrect.

NARRATOR: The girls tried not to make any noise, but they were excited that the sides were even now.

MISS PINKHAM: Sarah Sitwellington, the word goes to you. Tweezers.

SARAH: Tweezers . . . eh . . . t-w-e-e-z-i-r-s.

MISS PINKHAM: Incorrect, Sarah.

NARRATOR: When it was John's turn to spell the word, he started to wheeze.

MISS PINKHAM: Should you go to the nurse for some medication?

JOHN: No . . . I'm . . . okay. Uh, tweezers. T-w-e-z-o-r-s.

MISS PINKHAM: Incorrect, you'll have to sit down.

JOHN: I think I'm wheezing.

MISS PINKHAM: Then please go to the nurse.

NARRATOR: Herbie and Annabelle were the only ones left. The class didn't move.

MISS PINKHAM: Annabelle, your word is the same as the others. Tweezers.

ANNABELLE: I know, Miss Pinkham. Would you please use it in a sentence.

HERBIE: (To audience.) I know she's just stalling.

ANNABELLE: (Glares at Herbie.)

MISS PINKHAM: He used the tweezers to get the splinter out.

ANNABELLE: Tweezers . . . (To audience.) Does it end with an e-r or o-r? I'm not sure. I can't remember seeing that word anywhere. Here I go! (Clears throat.) Tweezers . . . t-w-e-e-z . . . o-r-s.

MISS PINKHAM: Incorrect.

BOYS: (Jump up.) YEAH!

MISS PINKHAM: (Claps hands twice.) JUST A MINUTE! Herbie Jones must spell the word correctly for the boys to win.

ANNABELLE: (Big smile at everyone.) How can Herbie spell it if I can't?

MISS PINKHAM: Spell tweezers, Herbie.

HERBIE: Tweezers. T-w-e-e . . .

ANNABELLE: (To audience.) He'll miss!

HERBIE: z . . .

ANNABELLE: (Shakes head.) He'll never get the ending right.

HERBIE: e . . . r . . . s.

ANNABELLE: Oh no!

MISS PINKHAM: Correct!

BOYS: (Cheer.) YAHOO!

NARRATOR: Annabelle walked up to Herbie.

ANNABELLE: You MUST have cheated, Herbie Jones. You knew that word was going to be given. Tweezers was NEVER on any of our spelling lists and not once was it in any of our stories. How could you have known?

HERBIE: I got lucky. Remember these? (Pulls out something from back pocket.) I carry these tweezers around with me all the time. The word tweezers is printed right on the side. I've been looking at that word for two years.

ANNABELLE: Eewyew! You use those awful tweezers to pick up spider eggs and . . . aaaugh, hairs in your food. HERBIE JONES, I'll never be your girlfriend as long as I live!

HERBIE: That's the nicest thing you've ever said to me.

ANNABELLE: It is, huh? (Flares her nostrils.) What do you think of this? I just put *two* check marks after your name on my memo pad.

HERBIE: Ahhhh . . . it's great to be back in check city.

Part Three
Herbie Jones
and the Class Gift

1

The Class Gift

Characters: Herbie Jones
Annabelle Louisa Hodgekiss
Raymond Martin
John Greenweed

Phillip McDoogle
Margie Sherman
Narrator

Setting: Classroom

Time: Two days in June

HERBIE: Why does it have to rain during recess? Guess I'll read my library book.

ANNABELLE: (Claps hands.) I want everyone's attention. (Pauses.) Raymond Martin!

RAYMOND: I'm busy drawing a Viking ship.

ANNABELLE: Put down your purple crayon. I have something important to say, and I am telling you now because the teacher is out of the room.

101

HERBIE: Ooooh . . . TOP SECRET!

ANNABELLE: Are you through oohing, Herbie Jones?

HERBIE: Ooooooh . . .

ANNABELLE: HERBIE!

HERBIE: I had to get one more in.

ANNABELLE: (Clears throat.) NOW, the last day of school many of us give Miss Pinkham a gift, like a coffee cup or . . .

JOHN: Some fudge . . . I even make it myself.

PHILLIP: I was painting "World's Best Teacher" on a piece of wood.

ANNABELLE: Well, I think we should do things differently this year.

RAYMOND: Me too. I don't think we have to give her anything.

MARGIE: Raymond! You're making Annabelle mad. Look, she's flaring her nostrils.

ANNABELLE: (Sniffs deeply and exhales.)

HERBIE: We could make one big class card and have everybody sign it.

ANNABELLE: A card isn't enough, Herbie. But we will need one. You can write a poem for it.

HERBIE: Okay, Annabelle, what's *your* big idea?

ANNABELLE: I was thinking we could all chip in a dollar and get Miss Pinkham one class gift.

JOHN: Who would pick it out?

ANNABELLE: Me.

JOHN: You? How come?

ANNABELLE: Because *I* have seen the inside of Miss Pinkham's house.

ALL: You have?

ANNABELLE: That was last month when I delivered some Girl Scout cookies. I happen to know Miss Pinkham collects ceramic owls. And . . . I saw a beautiful ceramic owl at Martha's House of Gifts on Main Street for about twenty-five dollars.

RAYMOND: Twenty-five dollars! Man, that's a lot of moola!

ANNABELLE: Not if we each contribute one dollar.

HERBIE: Wait a minute. Ray has a point. Twenty-five dollars *is* a lot of money. My dad always said the best gifts are the ones you make yourself . . . like John's fudge and Phillip's sign.

RAYMOND: Hey! Gifts from the liver are the best kind!

ANNABELLE: Gifts from the *liver?* Blaaugh! You mean gifts from the *heart.*

ALL: (Laugh.)

HERBIE: Listen, you guys, the liver and heart are practically next to each other. It's like saying the same thing.

RAYMOND: Yeah.

MARGIE: I'm tired of talking about hearts and livers. I like the owl gift. And Annabelle said Miss Pinkham collects them. I make a motion that we accept Annabelle's idea to bring in one dollar for Miss Pinkham's end-of-the-year gift.

ANNABELLE: . . . by Friday.

MARGIE: . . . by Friday.

ANNABELLE: Is there a second?

HERBIE: You want to buy *two?*

ANNABELLE: All in favor, say "aye."

ALL (Except Herbie and Raymond): AYE.

ANNABELLE: Opposed, say "nay."

HERBIE/RAYMOND: NAY!

ANNABELLE: Twenty-six to two. The majority wins! We will get Miss Pinkham one big class gift.

ALL (Except Herbie and Raymond): (Cheer and clap.)

NARRATOR: Annabelle held up her hand to quiet the class.

ANNABELLE: I will start collecting your dollars *tomorrow.* And . . . I'll make sure the *only* people who sign our card are the ones who paid their dollar contribution.

NARRATOR: After school, Herbie and Ray walked home in the drizzling rain.

RAYMOND: Annabelle is so bossy. She always gets her way.

HERBIE: Always.

RAYMOND: Can you loan me a dollar for that owl? I don't want to be the only one not signing the class card. Miss Pinkham's nice. She says I draw real good.

HERBIE: You're worried about this class gift business, aren't you?

RAYMOND: You're lucky, Herbie, both your parents work and they get along. My dad, well, he got laid off last week, and things haven't been very good. My parents argue a lot about money.

HERBIE: I feel bad about your dad losing his job. Listen, Ray, we can earn the money.

RAYMOND: We can? How?

HERBIE: I've got lots of old bottles in my basement. We can rinse them out and haul them down to Price Busters for a deposit.

RAYMOND: Sounds like a foolproof plan.

NARRATOR: The next morning in the classroom, Annabelle met Herbie at the door.

ANNABELLE: Did you write the poem for the teacher's gift?

HERBIE: Sure did. Here, read it.

ANNABELLE: This is a rhyme
At the end of the year
To say you are nice
And sweet.
Enjoy your vacation—
Read some good books,

Sit down and
Put up your feet.

I like it! It rhymes! It's even *spelled* correctly.

HERBIE: I had my sister check the spelling.

ANNABELLE: By the way, I've collected twenty-six dollars for the gift so far. Don't you and Ray want to contribute?

HERBIE: Sure. Right, Ray?

RAYMOND: I . . . I . . .

HERBIE: Excuse us, Annabelle. (Whispering.) Ray, what's the problem?

RAYMOND: Remember yesterday when we cashed in those forty bottles at Price Busters and you went home and I went home?

HERBIE: Yeah. I let you keep the deposit money until today.

RAYMOND: Well, I sort of . . . took a shortcut home.

HERBIE: So?

RAYMOND: By Burger Paradise.

HERBIE: Oh, no. You didn't . . .

RAYMOND: I smelled those cheeseburgers, Herbie, and I couldn't help myself. I *had* to go in.

HERBIE: YOU SPENT OUR MONEY FOR MISS PINK-HAM'S GIFT ON A CHEESEBURGER?

RAYMOND: No. (Pauses.) On Bits O'Chicken.

HERBIE: BITS O'CHICKEN? How could you do such a 'thing?

RAYMOND: I was hungry so . . . I got the nine-pack.

HERBIE: You're *always* hungry!

RAYMOND: . . . with the barbecue sauce.

HERBIE: Don't tell me any more!

ANNABELLE: You boys don't have your dollar contributions?

HERBIE: No.

ANNABELLE: Well, it wouldn't be fair if I let you sign the card. You haven't paid your dollars. Sorry.

HERBIE: (To audience.) Bits O'Chicken! Raymond makes me so mad! I feel like giving him something to eat. A knuckle sandwich! (Punches his hand hard.)

The M&Ms Fight

Characters: Narrator   Saleslady
            Raymond Martin   SFX Person
            Herbie Jones

Settings: Martha's House of Gifts; Main Street

Time: Saturday morning

NARRATOR: When Herbie and Ray arrived at the gift shop on Main Street, they peered inside the glass window. The boys suddenly felt uneasy about going inside.

RAYMOND: Gee, Herbie, this is a rich place. Just look at that thick pink rug. There's not one spot on it.

NARRATOR: Herbie read the sign on the door.

HERBIE: This is the place all right. It's Martha's House of Gifts. Why did Annabelle have to ask *us* to do this?

RAYMOND: (In a sarcastic voice.) Because *she* had a dentist appointment. I hope she gets drilled good.

HERBIE: (Laughs.) Okay, Ray. Let's go inside. All we have to do is pick up the teacher's end-of-the-year gift, and pay for the gift wrapping with *my mom's* two dollars.

NARRATOR: Herbie wanted Ray to know he hadn't forgotten that Ray had spent their hard-earned cash at Burger Paradise. Lucky for them, Herbie's mother bailed them out.

HERBIE: Come on, Ray, let's go inside.

SALESLADY: May I help you?

HERBIE: Yes. We're here to pick up an owl for our class.

SALESLADY: Hmmmmm, I remember seeing an owl behind the cash register. Here it is.

HERBIE: We want to buy a gift box for it, please.

SALESLADY: We have three kinds of fancy gift boxes on the shelf. Which one would you like?

BOYS: THAT ONE!

NARRATOR: The boys pointed to a purple box with white boats. The saleslady pulled it down from the shelf.

SALESLADY: I'll pack this owl very carefully now in some pink tissue paper and place it inside the box. There! Here's your gift!

HERBIE: Thank you. Here's our two dollar bills.

SALESLADY: I just need one. We have a special on gift boxes this weekend.

RAYMOND: Great! Then, I'll take that extra dollar.

NARRATOR: Herbie was smiling when the saleslady handed him the gift, but he was not smiling when he followed Ray out the door.

HERBIE: Ray, where do you think you're going with that dollar?

RAYMOND: Man, Herbie. I'm starved. Can't we spend it on some candy?

HERBIE: Gee, I don't know, Ray. That's really the class money.

RAYMOND: Look, we got a gift box that's worth two dollars. Who cares if we got it on special?

HERBIE: Hmmmm. The class gift is paid for. The gift box is paid for. What else do we need to buy?

RAYMOND: Candy!

NARRATOR: The boys raced down several blocks to the drug-store where they had the best selection.

HERBIE/RAYMOND: M&Ms!

NARRATOR: After the boys paid for the candy, they headed down Main Street.

RAYMOND: I'll count the M&Ms so we can divide them even Steven.

HERBIE: I'll count 'em.

RAYMOND: (Grumbling.) Herbert Dwight Jones, I am count-ing them.

HERBIE: (Grumbling.) Raymond Orville Martin, I AM COUNTING THE M&Ms.

SFX PERSON: (Slaps legs.)

RAYMOND: Herbie, you pushed me!

SFX PERSON: (Slaps legs again.)

HERBIE: Ray, you pushed me!

SFX PERSON: (Pounds fist in hand.)

RAYMOND: OUCH! You just knocked me into a parking me-ter! Why, you . . .

NARRATOR: Ray pushed Herbie so hard, the gift box Herbie was carrying popped out of his arms.

SFX PERSON: (Whistles, high to low, then makes a crash sound.)

RAYMOND: Oh no!

HERBIE: Look what you did!

RAYMOND: Me? You pushed me first.

HERBIE: The teacher's gift is broken in hundreds of tiny pieces.

RAYMOND: WE'RE DOOMED! The class will kill us. They expect an owl to come out of this box.

HERBIE: A twenty-five-dollar owl.

RAYMOND: All we have is a quarter. Where are we going to get an owl THAT CHEAP?

NARRATOR: The boys looked up the street.

BOYS: THE THRIFT SHOP!

RAYMOND: It's our only chance.

HERBIE: It's a real long shot.

3

Home Sweet Home

Characters: Narrator   SFX Person
Herbie Jones   Olivia Jones
Raymond Martin

Settings: Thrift shop; Herbie's house

Time: Saturday afternoon

NARRATOR: Herbie and Raymond took the empty gift box and raced into the thrift store.

HERBIE: What a big room! Look at all the knickknacks!

RAYMOND: Here's a neat alligator.

HERBIE: It's gotta be an OWL, Raymond. We have to find a ceramic owl for the teacher's gift. We broke it, remember?

RAYMOND: Couldn't it be an owligator?

HERBIE: Nice try, Ray. Keep looking.

RAYMOND: I FOUND ONE! I FOUND ONE!

HERBIE: Let me have it.

RAYMOND: See, it's got an owl on it.

HERBIE: Hmmmmm, but what's the owl sitting on? And what are these grooves? Wait a minute, Ray. This is an ASHTRAY! We can't give the teacher an ashtray. You know what she thinks about smoking.

RAYMOND: Yeah, she showed us a film once about a dragon who smoked. He turned green.

HERBIE: Maybe . . . maybe if we put our M&Ms in the ashtray, Miss Pinkham would think it was a candy dish.

RAYMOND: Not the M&Ms. I was looking forward to eating those.

HERBIE: Listen, Ray, we wouldn't be in this situation if it weren't for your stomach.

NARRATOR: After the boys paid a quarter for the gift, they went to Herbie's house. As soon as they got inside Herbie's bedroom, they opened up the big bag of M&Ms and poured them into the ashtray.

RAYMOND: Look at those M&Ms . . . Do you 'spose those candies are fresh?

HERBIE: (Sniffs deeply.) Smells okay to me. Why?

RAYMOND: Well, wouldn't it be awful if we gave the teacher stale candy? (Pauses.) Do you think we should try some to be sure?

HERBIE: No way, Raymond Orville Martin. I don't trust you when it comes to your stomach.

SFX PERSON: (Makes a stomach gurgling noise.)

HERBIE: Speaking of stomachs, excuse mine. I didn't have breakfast.

RAYMOND: Just one, Herbie?

HERBIE: Well . . . how could one M&M hurt? Okay. *One* brown M&M. Each.

RAYMOND: Mmmmmmmmm, that hits the spot.

HERBIE: Mmmmmm. Deeeeeelicious. Okay, let's close the lid now.

RAYMOND: Do you 'spose the green ones are fresh?

HERBIE: Huh?

RAYMOND: Maybe they make the brown ones fresh, but what about the green ones?

HERBIE: What about the red, yellow and tan ones then?

RAYMOND: Maybe we better taste ALL the colors . . . just to be on the safe side.

NARRATOR: Herbie started to drool.

SFX PERSON: (Makes a slurping noise.)

NARRATOR: And then Herbie did it without thinking. He popped a green candy, a red one and then a tan one into his mouth.

SFX PERSON: Mmmmmmmm! Mmmmm!

NARRATOR: While Herbie thought about seconds, Ray took huge handfuls of candy.

SFX PERSON: (Makes knocking noise.)

OLIVIA: HERBIE!

HERBIE: What do you want, Olive?

OLIVIA: Someone is here to see you.

HERBIE: Who?

OLIVIA: Annabelle Louisa Hodgekiss. Her dad is waiting for her in the car. She came to pick up some gift for the teacher.

HERBIE: Oh no! There's just one yellow M&M in the ashtray. How could I let this happen?

OLIVIA: HURRY UP!

HERBIE: Quick, Ray. Hand me the tape. I'm taping this lid three times.

RAYMOND: No problem, Herbie.

HERBIE: Wipe the chocolate off your mouth.

OLIVIA: HERBIE JONES, Annabelle's father is waiting.

HERBIE: I'm finished. What do you think, Ray?

RAYMOND: No one is going to get that baby open. Not even Miss Pinkham.

4

Herbie and Raymond in Church

Characters: SFX Person   Olivia Jones
Raymond Martin   Mrs. Jones
Herbie Jones   Mr. Jones
Narrator   Minister

Settings: Herbie's house; church

Time: Sunday morning

Prop: One sheet of paper rolled up

SFX PERSON: Brrrrrring! Brrrrrring!

RAYMOND: (Sleepy voice.) Yeah . . . ?

HERBIE: 992? This is Double 030.

119

RAYMOND: What are you calling so early for?

HERBIE: I'm gettin' worried about that twenty-five-cent gift we bought for the teacher at the thrift shop. Miss Pinkham's going to take one look at that thing and think it's an owl ashtray. One yellow M&M is not going to make her think it's a candy dish.

RAYMOND: So what do you have in mind?

HERBIE: I think we should go to church.

RAYMOND: HUH?

HERBIE: Listen, Ray, our minister said that when two or more people pray about the same thing, powerful things can happen. We need help to get out of this mess.

RAYMOND: You want me to pray with you?

HERBIE: In church. Can you get over here by ten?

RAYMOND: I don't have a tie.

HERBIE: You can borrow one of my dad's. Just get over here.

NARRATOR: At nine-thirty, the Joneses were going around the house shouting.

OLIVIA: Who took my brush?

MRS. JONES: Did anyone see my high-heeled shoes? I looked everywhere.

MR. JONES: (Hums a tune.)

MRS. JONES: MY RED HIGH HEEL! WHERE IS IT?

MR. JONES: (Calmly.) Is this what you were looking for, dear? I think you were using it last week to make a point. Or was it a heel? Anyway, it was thrown under the table.

NARRATOR: Mrs. Jones grabbed the shoe.

MRS. JONES: Do you think this dress is too tight on me? I simply can't eat any more donuts this month. I'm starting to wear them on my hips!

MR. JONES: Well, dear, they look better on you than they do in the display case.

NARRATOR: Mrs. Jones blushed. Just as they hugged, there was a knock on the back porch door.

SFX PERSON: (Knocks on desk.)

HERBIE: Hi, Ray!

RAYMOND: This suit okay? I wore it two years ago when I was the ring bearer in my cousin's wedding.

HERBIE: (Laughing.) I like your yellow socks. You look fine, Ray. Here, have a brown tie.

OLIVIA: Brown and blue? Aauugh!

HERBIE: Let's go!

NARRATOR: As the Joneses and Ray found seats in the last row of church, the choir was singing. When the music stopped, a man in a black robe got up to speak.

RAYMOND: Is that God?

HERBIE: No, dummy, that's the minister. God's in heaven . . . and . . . on earth.

RAYMOND: Well, if He's on earth, that means we must bump into Him sometimes.

OLIVIA: SHHHH! Don't talk in church!

NARRATOR: When the minister held up his hands for prayer, Herbie leaned over and whispered.

HERBIE: Now, remember, we're asking God to help us get out of this class gift mess. Maybe . . . maybe with His help, Miss Pinkham might like the gift.

RAYMOND: Should we tell Him we're sorry about fighting and breaking the teacher's owl?

HERBIE: It wouldn't hurt. You might throw in the Bits O'Chicken while you're at it.

MINISTER: Let us pray!

NARRATOR: The congregation was quiet. Everyone bowed their heads. After a minute, Ray sat up.

RAYMOND: I'm finished.

OLIVIA: SHHHH!

HERBIE: Think of something else. Just talk to Him.

NARRATOR: Ray shrugged and then bowed his head again like Herbie.

MINISTER: And now we will receive your tithes and offerings.

NARRATOR: Ray took off his tie, wadded it up and laid it on the tray.

HERBIE: You gave God a tie?

RAYMOND: Well, your minister said he was collecting 'em.

HERBIE: Not those kind, Raymond. He said *tithes* and offerings. And that wasn't *your* tie. It was my dad's!

NARRATOR: Herbie started to wonder if bringing Raymond to church was such a good idea. After the service was over, they walked out.

RAYMOND: Well, we got to talk to God about that class gift mess.

HERBIE: Yeah. He knows we need Him now.

RAYMOND: And you know, Herbie, since I had a little time left, I asked God if He could make the fish bite a little more on Saturday mornings.

HERBIE: Where's my church program!

NARRATOR: Herbie rolled it up and hit Raymond over the head.

SFX PERSON: (Hits desk with paper roll three times.)

RAYMOND: *OW!* Ow! Ow!

5

Doomsday

Characters: Narrator   Annabelle Louisa Hodgekiss
             Herbie Jones   John Greenweed
             Raymond Martin   Miss Pinkham

Setting: Classroom

Time: Last day of school

NARRATOR: Herbie and Ray stood in the hallway as they talked about what they brought for the end-of-the-year party.

HERBIE: What are those?

RAYMOND: Pickled beet slices.

HERBIE: Pickled what?

RAYMOND: Beet slices. Mom buys them all the time. She says they can be partyish, too.

NARRATOR: Herbie rolled his eyeballs. He was glad his mother was not like Mrs. Martin.

RAYMOND: What did you bring?

HERBIE: Annabelle signed me up for punch three weeks ago. So that's what I'm bringing for today's class party.

RAYMOND: What kind?

HERBIE: (Smiles.) Adam's Ale.

RAYMOND: YOU BROUGHT A WHOLE GALLON JUG OF WATER TO OUR PARTY?

HERBIE: Yup.

RAYMOND: I don't believe you, Herbie.

HERBIE: Hey, soda's expensive. My mom gave us the two dollars for the teacher's gift. I told her we didn't need soda this week.

RAYMOND: Well, right after Miss Pinkham sees my great picture on the class card, and she reads your great poem, we cut out the door, right, Herbie?

HERBIE: Yeah . . . unless . . . our prayers worked.

RAYMOND: I don't know. It looks like doomsday for us. As soon as the class finds out we broke the teacher's owl and put a twenty-five-cent owl ashtray in that gift box, we'll be doomed.

HERBIE: You're probably right, Ray. Plan on hightailing it out of there with me.

NARRATOR: When the boys walked into the classroom, Annabelle came right over to them.

ANNABELLE: Oh, Herbie, I am so thrilled about our class gift, I can't wait. Can you? Hmmmmmmmmmmmmm?

HERBIE: (Grumbles something.)

ANNABELLE: Why, Herbie, you seem mad. Something bothering you, hmmmmmmmmmmmmm?

NARRATOR: Annabelle's "hmmmm"s were starting to bother Herbie. John Greenweed came into the room with a giant plastic bag of popcorn.

JOHN: Glad you brought a gallon jug of punch, Herbie. Popcorn makes me thirsty.

HERBIE: (To himself.) Wait till they taste my Adam's Ale.

NARRATOR: A moment later Miss Pinkham walked into the classroom. When she saw the flowers and the gift, she clapped her hands.

MISS PINKHAM: Oh! What's all this?

ANNABELLE: It's a gift for you . . . from the class.

MISS PINKHAM: My goodness! How thoughtful! How did you plan all this without my knowing about it?

ANNABELLE: It wasn't easy.

MISS PINKHAM: What a wonderful Viking ship. Did Raymond draw that?

RAYMOND: I sure did. Do you like the helmet I put on your head?

MISS PINKHAM: Is that me?

RAYMOND: You're the captain!

MISS PINKHAM: I love it! How thoughtful you were to draw this, Ray. And I like how everyone wrote their full names.

ANNABELLE: That was my idea.

MISS PINKHAM: Ooooh, there's a poem inside. Did you write it, Annabelle? It looks like your handwriting.

ANNABELLE: It *is* my handwriting. I copied the poem over for neatness, but I didn't write it.

HERBIE: (To himself.) Gee, I was hoping Annabelle would tell Miss Pinkham I wrote it. I feel funny telling her myself.

MISS PINKHAM: Hmmmm, then it must be Herbie Jones because he loves to write poems. Am I right, Herbie?

HERBIE: (Big smile.) You're right!

ANNABELLE: Open the gift, Miss Pinkham.

HERBIE/RAYMOND: (Groan.)

MISS PINKHAM: Ooooh, I love the purple sailboats on the gift box! And look at the fancy pink tissue paper inside. My goodness, what could this be?

HERBIE: (To himself.) Why was it so easy for her to take the lid off? I taped three rows of tape around that thing. (To Annabelle.) Did you take the tape off?

ANNABELLE: Uh-huh. Is this yours?

HERBIE: (Eyes bulge.) THE YELLOW M&M! You *know*! And now . . . (Gulps and points at the teacher.) She's gonna know.

RAYMOND: We better cut out of here, Herbie.

MISS PINKHAM: HOW BEAUTIFUL!

HERBIE/RAYMOND: BEAUTIFUL?

MISS PINKHAM: Just look at this beautiful ceramic owl! How did you know that I collect them?

RAYMOND: Herbie, *that's* the owl we broke. But . . . it's not broken anymore.

HERBIE: How could that be?

MISS PINKHAM: Thank you, boys and girls! I'll treasure this gift and card.

RAYMOND: (To Herbie.) IT WAS A MIRACLE!

JOHN: Let's PARTY! I'll pass out my popcorn.

ANNABELLE: (To Herbie.) I can't *believe* you actually put an ashtray in that gift box for our teacher.

HERBIE: Where is the ashtray?

ANNABELLE: Martha's House of Gifts called me that same night to apologize for giving us the wrong owl.

HERBIE: The wrong owl?

ANNABELLE: The one with the crack in the back. It was lucky I filled out the bottom part of that sales slip with my name and address. She was able to get in touch with me. Before I went down, I opened up your gift box. I was shocked.

HERBIE: (Big sigh.) I'm relieved.

ANNABELLE: Listen, sleazeball, I was just lucky that I didn't have to return the owl with the crack in it. The saleslady said she didn't want it. So I took that awful ashtray and threw it in the trash.

HERBIE: Why didn't you tell me before?

ANNABELLE: Because I . . . wanted you to *suffer*. You deserved some punishment for trying to pawn off a used gift like that on our teacher.

HERBIE: (Another sigh.) It's over!

JOHN: Popcorn?

ANNABELLE: I'm thirsty. Who was supposed to bring the punch?

HERBIE: (Big smile.) I was. May I pour you some?

ANNABELLE: Why, Herbie Jones, your manners are improving.

RAYMOND: This'll be good.

HERBIE: It's called . . . "Adam's Ale."

ANNABELLE: What a wonderful name. Is it like ginger ale? I love that.

HERBIE: No, it has a taste of its own. I think you can best appreciate it if you close your eyes when you drink it.

ANNABELLE: Okay, I'm closing my eyes.

HERBIE: No peeking.

ANNABELLE: Herbie Jones, I never peek! Now, let me take a sip of that Adam's Ale.

HERBIE: (Singing.) Be my guest!

ANNABELLE: I like trying new things. Adam's Ale. Hmmm. Gulp, gulp, gulp. (Eyes bulge open.) HERBIE JONES! YOU BROUGHT WATER TO OUR END-OF-THE-YEAR PARTY!

Part Four

Herbie Jones
and the Monster Ball

1

The First
Baseball Practice

Characters: Narrator   Annabelle Louisa Hodgekiss
            Raymond Martin   John Greenweed
            Herbie Jones   Margie Sherman
            Uncle Dwight   SFX Person
            Phillip McDoogle

Setting: Laurel Woods Park

Time: Summer morning

NARRATOR: Herbie and Ray arrived at the park wearing their Laurel Beef baseball caps. After they parked their bikes, they walked slowly across the green.

RAYMOND: Look what a big shot your uncle is! He's carrying a clipboard and has a whistle around his neck.

HERBIE: Hey! That's John Greenweed, Phillip McDoogle, Margie Sherman and Annabelle Louisa Hodgekiss over there with him. All the kids from school are on the team. I'm gettin' out of here.

NARRATOR: Herbie ran for his bike.

UNCLE DWIGHT: HEY, BOYS! OVER HERE!

HERBIE: (Groans.) It's too late.

NARRATOR: Slowly, Herbie and Ray walked across the green.

PHILLIP: Oh no! Look who's coming. Now we'll never win a game.

ANNABELLE: They're instant outs at school.

UNCLE DWIGHT: Okay, kids, gather around. I want you to meet two more members of our team. This is Ray Martin, otherwise known as Mr. Baseball.

ALL: Mr. Baseball?

UNCLE DWIGHT: And this . . . is my nephew Herbie.

ALL: *Your* nephew?

ANNABELLE: My dad thought you two might be related, Coach Jones. I just . . . didn't believe him.

NARRATOR: Herbie took off his cap and fiddled with it.

ANNABELLE: I like your hats, boys. Gold is my favorite color.

RAYMOND: (Whispers.) How come she's so friendly?

HERBIE: (Whispers.) My uncle is the coach.

UNCLE DWIGHT: Okay, kids, let's start practice. The first thing we have to do is very important.

JOHN: What's the first thing?

UNCLE DWIGHT: We have to sing.

ALL: Sing?

UNCLE DWIGHT: Sure. At your age, baseball should be fun. I want to make sure we start each practice on a good note. So, before we do anything else, I'm going to lead you in a very important song. You know the words. Sing along with me. Hmmmmmm.

Take me out to the ball game . . .

ALL: (Sing rest of song.)
Take me out with the crowd.
Buy me some peanuts and Cracker Jack!
I don't care if I never get back.

Oh it's root, root, root for the home team,
If they don't win, it's a shame.
For it's one, two, three strikes you're out
At the old ball game!

UNCLE DWIGHT: Now we have an important second thing
to do.

MARGIE: Is it as much fun as the first?

UNCLE DWIGHT: Wait and see.

NARRATOR: Uncle Dwight brought out a big brown bag.

RAYMOND: REFRESHMENTS!

UNCLE DWIGHT: Help yourself to some roasted peanuts
while I talk to you about baseball.

ALL: (Cheer and clap.)

NARRATOR: Herbie took out a notepad from his back pocket.

HERBIE: "How to Be a Baseball Great." I better take notes.

UNCLE DWIGHT: First, you have to have enthusiasm and
want to do your best.

RAYMOND: GO LAUREL WOODS PARK! GO! GO! GO!

UNCLE DWIGHT: That's the idea, Raymond.

RAYMOND: You're lookin' at Captain Hustle.

JOHN/PHILLIP: (Crack up.)

RAYMOND: GO! GO! GO! This baseball business is gonna be a cinch.

HERBIE: "Enthusiasm." I'm writing that down.

UNCLE DWIGHT: Okay, kids. You know we have one hour of practice each morning at the park. Well, the real practice is what YOU do on your own. Find someone to play catch with. Practice your throwing.

NARRATOR: Herbie continued writing.

HERBIE: "Practice on your own."

UNCLE DWIGHT: The third thing I want to tell you is, don't give up!

HERBIE: "Don't . . . give . . . up."

UNCLE DWIGHT: Okay, let's have some batting practice.

ANNABELLE: I'm up first.

PHILLIP: Look at Annabelle. She thinks she's a baseball great.

ANNABELLE: Knee bends . . . breathe in, breathe out . . . smooth batting gloves . . . line up my knuckles on the bat . . .

UNCLE DWIGHT: You've been well coached.

ANNABELLE: My dad worked with me. I'm ready!

SFX PERSON: Blam! Wham! CRACK!

PHILLIP: Annabelle is a slugger!

NARRATOR: When it was Ray's turn at bat, everyone in the field lay down.

JOHN: I'm using second base as a pillow. (Snores.) Han shooo . . . Han shooo . . .

UNCLE DWIGHT: Get up and play ball! This is not nap time.

NARRATOR: Ray hit the first ball. It was a nubber and rolled three feet.

UNCLE DWIGHT: Don't take any more golf swings, Ray. Swing level like this.

SFX PERSON: BLAM!

NARRATOR: Ray grounded the ball to third base.

RAYMOND: YAHOO! LAUREL WOODS PARK! I'm a hitter!

HERBIE: Now I feel worse. I'm the only guy around here that can't hit.

UNCLE DWIGHT: Okay, slugger, here comes your first pitch.

NARRATOR: Uncle Dwight wound up and delivered a ball.

HERBIE: Oh, gee . . . here it comes.

SFX PERSON: WHIFFF!

PHILLIP: (Whispering.) I told you he was a loser.

NARRATOR: Uncle Dwight ran over and checked Herbie's batting stance.

UNCLE DWIGHT: Hold your bat back, Herbie. Get that elbow up. Watch the ball.

NARRATOR: Coach Jones pitched again.

SFX PERSON: WHIFFF!

HERBIE: Why do I keep missing?

PHILLIP: We've got a real Captain Whiff at the plate.

JOHN/PHILLIP: (Laugh.)

NARRATOR: Herbie's eyes started to fill up with tears. Quickly he wiped them with his sleeve.

HERBIE: (To himself.) I can hardly see the ball now.

UNCLE DWIGHT: We can work on your hitting tomorrow, slugger. Okay, kids, practice is over.

PHILLIP: (Whispers.) Hey, John and Annabelle. Everyone can hit on this team but Herbie. And he's the coach's nephew.

HERBIE: I know they're talking about me, but I'll show them. (Sniffs a few times.) I'm practicing every day in my backyard.

2

Sleigh Bells

Characters: Narrator Uncle Dwight
Mrs. Jones SFX Person
Herbie Jones Raymond Martin
Mr. Jones

Setting: Herbie's house

Time: Summer morning

NARRATOR: It was Thursday morning and Mrs. Jones was rushing around getting ready for work at Dipping Donuts. She opened the door to the attic stairs and hollered for the second time.

MRS. JONES: DWIGHT JONES! I HAVE TO LEAVE IN FIVE MINUTES. IF YOU WANT AN EGG, YOU BETTER GET DOWN HERE. NOW.

NARRATOR: Herbie picked up a grape off the kitchen table and tried to hit it with his spoon.

143

MRS. JONES: Your uncle can be impossible at times. What are you doing, Herbie?

HERBIE: Practicing my hitting.

MRS. JONES: DWIGHT JONES!

NARRATOR: Mr. Jones peeked his head around the corner.

MR. JONES: (Grumbling.) I have to get some shut-eye.

MRS. JONES: Well, I have to go to work. Here's the spatula. *You* can make your brother's breakfast.

NARRATOR: Mr. Jones looked at the spatula and yawned.

MR. JONES: (Big loud yawn.)

NARRATOR: Just then the attic door flew open, and Uncle Dwight walked into the kitchen. His shirt was untucked and his hair uncombed.

UNCLE DWIGHT: What time is it?

HERBIE: Nine o'clock.

UNCLE DWIGHT: NINE? I'm supposed to be at work now!

MR. JONES: You better take Olivia's bike and eat something on the way. I was going to cook you something. Got a hot griddle here.

NARRATOR: Dwight reached in his shirt pocket and pulled out two Twinkies.

UNCLE DWIGHT: How 'bout frying these up?

HERBIE: Man, fried Twinkies. Neato!

MR. JONES: (Grumbles.) Thanks, Dwight. After I get the cellophane off, I'll turn them a few times on the grill.

UNCLE DWIGHT: Flip 'em to me, brother!

NARRATOR: Mr. Jones shook his head as he flipped the fried Twinkies. Dwight caught one in each hand. Then he raced outside to the garage. Herbie ran out and watched his uncle leave.

UNCLE DWIGHT: See you at practice later this morning, Herbie.

HERBIE: (Groans.) Yeah.

UNCLE DWIGHT: Hey! We have a whole week before our first game. You're going to do fine. I'll teach you how to knit tonight. That'll relax you.

HERBIE: KNIT?

UNCLE DWIGHT: Sure. I belong to the Knit Wits. A bunch of us on the varsity team at UCONN knit before each game. It gives your mind a rest.

HERBIE: You're a weirdo, Uncle Dwight.

NARRATOR: Uncle Dwight smiled as he hopped on Olivia's bike, jumped on the seat and rode off.

HERBIE: Just look at him! He's got those Twinkies clenched between his teeth like two big cigars. (Pauses.) What a neat guy.

NARRATOR: Herbie watched his uncle round the corner, and then went back to the kitchen table and continued hitting grapes with his spoon.

HERBIE: BLAM! I got off a good one! Look at that thing go! Oooops!

MR. JONES: HERBIE JONES! THAT GRAPE JUST HIT MY HEAD! Stop foolin' around. I'm tired.

SFX PERSON: Bzzzzzzz. Bzzzzzzz.

NARRATOR: Herbie was saved by the doorbell. He ran to get it.

NARRATOR: It was Raymond. Herbie wasn't glad to see him. He grabbed his mitt and headed out the door.

RAYMOND: Are you mad?

HERBIE: Of course I'm mad. You cut out on me yesterday. We were supposed to play catch in my backyard together. *Remember?*

RAYMOND: Listen, Herbie. I spent all afternoon and evening going through my baseball card collection. I told you I'd help you and I can.

HERBIE: What are you talking about? You heard the coach. He said we have to practice every day on our own!

RAYMOND: Forget that. I have the formula. I know what makes a baseball great.

HERBIE: What formula? Is this another one of your dumb ideas?

RAYMOND: Look what I have in my hand.

HERBIE: Baseball cards.

RAYMOND: Yes, and look who's on them! The greatest ball players.

HERBIE: So?

RAYMOND: So, look at their names. All the greats have one sleigh bell names.

HERBIE: Sleigh bells?

RAYMOND: You know. Sounds. The word car has one sleigh bell. Baseball has two sleigh bells. We learned that in school a long time ago.

HERBIE: You mean syllables?

RAYMOND: Yeah, that's what they are! Listen to these greats with one sleigh bell names.

NARRATOR: Herbie listened closely. He wasn't mad anymore. Ray was trying to help him with baseball.

RAYMOND: Babe Ruth
Ty Cobb
Moose Haas
Fred Lynn
Jim Rice
Ron Cey
George Brett
Mike Schmidt
Cy Young
Pete Rose
Wade Boggs
Oil Can Boyd

And that's not all of them!

HERBIE: Hey! How 'bout that! They're the REAL greats and they have one-syllable names.

RAYMOND: Even your uncle's name is a baseball great! Dwight Jones! Now all we have to do is change our names.

HERBIE: How?

RAYMOND: You're Herb Jones—the baseball great!

HERBIE: Herb Jones? Herb Jones—the baseball great! I like it. But what about you—Raymond Martin?

RAYMOND: You're lookin' at another baseball great—Ray Mart.

HERBIE: Ray Mart? That sounds like K-Mart.

RAYMOND: Don't knock it, Herb, we're baseball greats now!

3

The Worst Sandwich

Characters: Narrator   Raymond Martin

              Herbie Jones   Miss Pinkham

              Shadow

Setting: The swimming hole

Time: Summer morning

NARRATOR: Herbie didn't feel like going to baseball practice even with his new one-syllable name.

HERBIE: Want to ride our bikes by the swimming hole, Ray Mart?

SHADOW: Ruf! Ruf!

RAYMOND: Sure, Herb Jones. Let's go, Shadow!

NARRATOR: As the boys rode along the river, Herbie heard something.

HERBIE: Did you hear that?

RAYMOND: What?

HERBIE: There's splashing coming from the swimming hole. Who would be swimming this early in the morning?

RAYMOND: This looks like an interesting spy mission, Double 030.

NARRATOR: The boys screeched their bikes to a halt and peeked over the bushes.

RAYMOND: It's a lady and she's wearing a bathing cap.

HERBIE: Uh oh! Shadow is sniffing that lady's lunch.

SHADOW: Sniff! Sniff! (Low growl.)

RAYMOND: Come back here, Shadow!

HERBIE: Look, he's got his nose in the bag!

RAYMOND: Over here, boy. Give it to me.

HERBIE: He pulled out a sandwich.

SHADOW: (Hungry growl.)

HERBIE: He's eating it!

NARRATOR: The boys dived on the dog, but it was too late. Shadow gulped the last bite.

SHADOW: (Smacks lips. Licks chops.)

RAYMOND: Great! Just great! Now what do we do?

HERBIE: We have to replace the sandwich. What kind was it?

RAYMOND: You're askin' me? I didn't eat it—he did!

HERBIE: Come here, Shadow. Let me smell your breath.

SHADOW: (Pants.)

HERBIE: Aaaaaaaaugh!

RAYMOND: What kind was it? Salami?

HERBIE: (Groans.) Worse than that.

RAYMOND: Egg?

HERBIE: It was liverwurst.

RAYMOND: Liverwurst? That IS the worst sandwich.

HERBIE: Where can we get some fast?

RAYMOND: Hmmmm, my dad loves the stuff. I bet I have

some in my fridge. I could put some on two slices of bread, pop it into a brown bag and be back here in five minutes.

HERBIE: You're amazing, Ray Mart. Get going. I'll guard the fort here.

NARRATOR: Herbie looked back at the lake.

HERBIE: The lady is going to dive off that big rock. There she goes. Wow! What a perfect dive. She swims like that movie star Esther Williams, on the late show.

NARRATOR: Five minutes later, the lady got out of the water.

HERBIE: (To himself.) What if she notices her lunch is gone? Hurry up, Ray. Now she's taking her bathing cap off. Wait a minute. I know that lady! It's . . . Miss Pinkham, my teacher from third grade. I'm covering my eyes. I shouldn't see my teacher in a bathing suit!

NARRATOR: Suddenly Ray showed up with Shadow and a brown bag.

RAYMOND: Why do you have your eyes closed?

HERBIE: We know that lady!

RAYMOND: We do? Oh, gee! It's Miss Pinkham. There she is asleep on the blanket.

NARRATOR: Herbie finally opened his eyes.

HERBIE: Did you bring a sandwich?

RAYMOND: Yeah. But we didn't have liverwurst in our refrigerator.

HERBIE: So what did you make?

RAYMOND: I made her a liver sandwich.

HERBIE: A LIVER SANDWICH?

RAYMOND: Shhh! She's still sleeping. She won't know the difference.

HERBIE: Well, let's replace this lunch bag and get out of here.

NARRATOR: As the boys tiptoed across the sandy riverbank, Shadow started barking.

SHADOW: Ruf! Ruf!

BOYS: Oh no!

NARRATOR: Just when the boys had dropped her lunch bag on her blanket, Miss Pinkham woke up.

MISS PINKHAM: Oh! Boys. What a surprise to see you.

HERBIE: We . . . we . . . we were in the neighborhood so we thought we would stop by and say hello.

RAYMOND: (Whispers.) You sound like my mother.

MISS PINKHAM: Sit down. I just finished a good morning swim. I had the river to myself.

RAYMOND: Just you and the tadpoles.

MISS PINKHAM: Eweyee, that makes me cringe. So . . . what have you boys been doing this summer?

RAYMOND: We've been spending lots of time in the library. We just love those psycho pedias.

HERBIE: (Jabs his buddy.)

MISS PINKHAM: I'm glad you're reading. You boys want part of my sandwich? I always get hungry after a swim.

HERBIE: Eh . . . we have to go now. Right, Ray?

RAYMOND: Right, Herb. Bye, Miss Pinkham.

MISS PINKHAM: Bye!

NARRATOR: Just as the boys got to their bikes they heard a shrill scream.

MISS PINKHAM: (Screams.)

HERBIE: That liver you put in her sandwich . . .

RAYMOND: Yeah?

HERBIE: It was cooked, wasn't it?

RAYMOND: I didn't have time. I just slid it right onto the bread, blood and all.

HERBIE: HOW COULD YOU?

NARRATOR: Herbie hopped on his bike and pedaled away.

RAYMOND: WAIT FOR ME!

4

A Talk with
the Monster Ball

Characters: Narrator   Uncle Dwight
               Olivia Jones   SFX Person
               Herbie Jones

Setting: Herbie's house

Time: Summer afternoon and evening

NARRATOR: Olivia came by and peeked her head in Herbie's room.

OLIVIA: You should have been down at the swimming hole, Erb. The water was great!

NARRATOR: Herbie looked up from his notebook.

HERBIE: I was.

157

OLIVIA: You were? I didn't see you. I was there since noon.

HERBIE: I was there this morning.

OLIVIA: You cut baseball practice?

HERBIE: I gotta work some more on my hitting before I show up again.

OLIVIA: ERB JONES, you are in big trouble!

HERBIE: I am?

OLIVIA: When you're on a team, you never miss a practice.

HERBIE: N-n-never?

OLIVIA: Not unless you're real sick. Uncle Dwight is going to be so mad!

NARRATOR: Ten minutes later, there was a knock on Herbie's door.

UNCLE DWIGHT: You there, Herbie?

HERBIE: Oh no, it's Uncle Dwight. He's probably going to be mad that I didn't go to practice.

UNCLE DWIGHT: Yoohoo, Herbie? Can I come in?

HERBIE: (Clears throat.) Eh . . . yeah. The door's not locked.

SFX PERSON: BLAM! Crash! (Claps hands once loudly.)

UNCLE DWIGHT: Whoooops! You didn't tell me you had a chair behind the door.

HERBIE: Sorry.

UNCLE DWIGHT: That's okay. What's up?

HERBIE: Nothing much.

UNCLE DWIGHT: Writing some poems?

HERBIE: A few.

UNCLE DWIGHT: That's great. Want to read some to the Monster Ball? And me? Come on.

NARRATOR: Herbie slowly followed his uncle upstairs to the attic room and sat down on the unmade bed. Uncle Dwight picked up the Monster Ball and sat on a chair.

UNCLE DWIGHT: Okay. We're ready for your first poem.

NARRATOR: Herbie opened his notebook and read one.

HERBIE: I like spiders
      And the way they crawl
      You can find them in dark places
      But not at the mall.

NARRATOR: Uncle Dwight held the Monster Ball up to his right ear.

UNCLE DWIGHT: He likes your poem. Do you have another one?

HERBIE: The lady can dive and
Swim real far
She looks like Esther Williams
The movie star.

NARRATOR: This time Uncle Dwight held the Monster Ball up to his left ear.

UNCLE DWIGHT: The Monster Ball really likes that poem. Now he wants to know why you didn't show up at practice today.

NARRATOR: Herbie closed his notepad. He didn't feel like talking.

UNCLE DWIGHT: Hmmmmm, I see.

NARRATOR: Uncle Dwight listened to the Monster Ball again.

HERBIE: What did he say?

UNCLE DWIGHT: He said you didn't want to go to practice because you thought you would just strike out again.

HERBIE: How did he know?

UNCLE DWIGHT: The Monster Ball knows all.

NARRATOR: Herbie didn't look at his uncle. He felt rotten about his hitting. And now he felt rotten about cutting practice. Herbie took out his pen and scribbled on the bottom of his shoe.

HERBIE: Do you think I stink as a baseball player?

UNCLE DWIGHT: No. You don't stink. You're learning. You're making progress. Yesterday you whiffed at every ball. Next time you'll get a piece. It's just a matter of time. But you have to come to practice. Our first game is Saturday against Beechwood.

HERBIE: Our first game!

UNCLE DWIGHT: Don't worry about striking out, Herbie. Everyone does. Even great batters like the Mighty Casey. Ever hear of him?

HERBIE: No.

UNCLE DWIGHT: You should. You're a poet. Just a minute, let me check my bookshelf. Here it is, "Casey at the Bat." Listen to this:

And now the pitcher holds the ball, and now he lets it go,
And now the air is shattered by the force of Casey's blow.

Oh, somewhere in this favored land the sun is shining
     bright,

The band is playing somewhere, and somewhere hearts are
     light;
And somewhere men are laughing, and somewhere
     children shout,
But there is no joy in Mudville—Mighty Casey has struck
     out.

HERBIE: Casey was a great ballplayer and he whiffed?

UNCLE DWIGHT: Yup.

HERBIE: He must have felt bad when it happened. (Pauses.)
Can I copy this poem in my notebook?

UNCLE DWIGHT: Sure, and why don't you try writing your
own baseball poem? Then I'll pitch you a few after I take
a nap.

HERBIE: You will?

UNCLE DWIGHT: (Yawns.) Sure, Herbie.

NARRATOR: While Uncle Dwight laid down on his bed with
the Monster Ball and fell asleep, Herbie took out his notebook, copied the poem about Casey and made two poems
of his own.

HERBIE: Finished! Let's see how they sound. (Reads them
to himself.):

          Cutting practice is a
          Dumb thing to do.

We're gonna beat Beechwood
So don't be blue.

My coach is tall.
My coach is nice.
He helps me play ball
And he eats lots of rice.

NARRATOR: Herbie left the two poems on Uncle Dwight's pillow. Then he watched his uncle snore for a few minutes before he tiptoed out.

UNCLE DWIGHT: Han shoo! Han shoo! Han shoooo!

HERBIE: I think I'll go in the backyard and practice throwing. Mom hung the clothes on the line, so I'll have some good targets. Let's see . . . I'll aim for that towel first.

NARRATOR: Herbie brought back his arm and hurled the ball.

SFX PERSON: WHOOOOOOSH! Booooooooooing!

HERBIE: Oh no! It landed smack in Olivia's purple bathing suit. The top part! (Looks around.) I'm sure glad no one saw me do that. Boy, do I need practice!

NARRATOR: That night Uncle Dwight pitched Herbie ninety balls at the park. Herbie missed forty-five of them. He got a piece of forty-three of them. And finally . . .

HERBIE: YAHOO! I hit two in right field!

NARRATOR: When Herbie got home, he returned to the backyard.

HERBIE: I'm throwing this ball at the clothesline till the moon comes out. And then I'm throwin' some more.

5

The Big Game

Characters: Uncle Dwight   John Greenwood
Phillip McDoogle   Olivia Jones
Herbie Jones   Mr. Jones
Raymond Martin   Mrs. Jones
Annabelle Louisa Hodgekiss   Margie Sherman
Narrator   Beechwood pitcher
Umpire   Beechwood fielder
SFX Person   Mr. Hodgekiss

Setting: Laurel Woods baseball diamond

Time: Summer. Noon on Saturday.

UNCLE DWIGHT: Well, team, *everyone* who showed up today for our big game against Beechwood (holds finger up)
is playing six full innings. Good thing we have twelve players on our roster. Two kids are on vacation and one is sick.

165

PHILLIP: (Groans.) That means Herbie has to bat at least three times. Boy, the air is gonna take a real beating today. Captain Whiff will be striking away!

HERBIE: (Puts his nose close to Phillip's.) Everyone strikes out sometime. Ever read the poem about Mighty Casey?

UNCLE DWIGHT: (Smiles at Herbie.) Okay, you guys, we're a team, RIGHT?

LAUREL BEEF TEAM: *RIGHT!*

UNCLE DWIGHT: Who are we gonna beat today?

LAUREL BEEF TEAM: *BEECHWOOD!*

UNCLE DWIGHT: And who are we?

LAUREL BEEF TEAM: *LAUREL BEEF!*

RAY MART: (Very loudly.) *Mooooooooo!*

ANNABELLE: Raymond! That's the sound a milk cow makes. We're *not* milk cows, we're the . . .

HERBIE: (Deep voice.) *BIG* BEEF.

HERBIE/RAY: *BIG* BEEF!

LAUREL BEEF TEAM: YEAH!

UNCLE DWIGHT: Okay, Beefers, this is it! Go outfield and play some BIG D!

LAUREL BEEF TEAM: DEFENSE!

ANNABELLE: (Raises hand.) Coach Jones, you said that we should sing first before each practice. I think we should sing before each game, too.

UNCLE DWIGHT: What a great idea, Annabelle. What song?

ANNABELLE: (Proudly.) I was thinking of our national anthem.

UNCLE DWIGHT: Let's do it!

ANNABELLE: (Clears throat.) Caps *off*, please. (Sounds first note.) Hmmmmmm.

ALL: (Everyone sings the national anthem.)

Oh, say can you see by the dawn's early light
What so proudly we hailed at the twilight's last gleaming?
Whose broad stripes and bright stars, thru the perilous
        fight,
O'er the ramparts we watched were so gallantly streaming?
And the rocket's red glare, the bombs bursting in air,
Gave proof through the night that our flag was still there.
Oh, say does that star-spangled banner yet wave
O'er the land of the free and the home of the brave?

NARRATOR: After the song, the umpire took a small whisk broom out of his back pocket and brushed off home plate.

UMPIRE: PLAY BALL!

SFX PERSON: *WHACK!*

NARRATOR: The starting batter for Beechwood hit a line drive to John Greenweed at second base.

JOHN: I GOT IT. (Socks hand.) Yeah!

UMPIRE: ONE AWAY!

LAUREL BEEF TEAM: (Cheer!)

NARRATOR: The next Beechwood batter smashed a grounder up the first-base line. Annabelle charged it.

ANNABELLE: I'm scooping this ball up right now with my glove and touching first. (Socks hand and then stamps foot.)

UMPIRE: HE'S OUT OF THERE! TWO AWAY!

LAUREL BEEF TEAM: (Cheer!)

ANNABELLE: I'm a vacuum cleaner at first base. No ball gets by me!

NARRATOR: The third Beechwood batter poked the ball into center field. Herbie ran for it.

HERBIE: This one's mine. I'm keeping my eye on the ball, and I'm squeezing my mitt just like Dad told me to. (Punches fist.)

UMPIRE: THREE AWAY!

HERBIE: (Looks into his glove.) It's in my mitt! I CAUGHT THE BALL! (Leaps in air.) YAHOO!

NARRATOR: Herbie's family hollered from the stands.

OLIVIA: THAT'S MY BROTHER!

MR. and MRS. JONES: THAT'S MY SON!

NARRATOR: As the game went on, both sides played good defense. But *now* it was the last inning, and Beechwood was ahead, 2–0. Laurel Beef had one more chance to score in the bottom of the sixth.

HERBIE: (Puts hand on his head.) Oh no! I think I'm up!

UNCLE DWIGHT: Okay, Beefers, it's the bottom of the batting order. Margie Sherman and Herbie Jones—you're up.

HERBIE: (Groans.) I *am* up . . . after Margie.

MARGIE: I'm ready! Pitch me something over the plate!

NARRATOR: The Beechwood pitcher smiled.

BEECHWOOD PITCHER: Here comes my fastball. Look out!

MARGIE: I'm creaming this ball!

SFX PERSON: BLAM!

PHILLIP: Look at Margie go! She's waving her hat in the air!

UMPIRE: SAFE AT SECOND!

LAUREL BEEF TEAM: (Cheer!)

HERBIE: Oh no, now it's *my* turn to bat.

UNCLE DWIGHT: Come on, Herbie, you can do it!

NARRATOR: Herbie's sister yelled from the bleachers.

OLIVIA: You did it before, Herbie, at the park! Remember?

HERBIE: (Groans.) Yeah . . . Uncle Dwight pitched me ninety balls and I hit two.

NARRATOR: The Beechwood first baseman started to laugh.

BEECHWOOD FIELDER: Heh! Heh! Heh! This is the guy who struck out *twice* before. *Easy out!*

BEECHWOOD PITCHER: I'm winding up. Here comes my fastball!

SFX PERSON: WHOOOSH!

HERBIE: (Groans.) Oh, I missed it!

UMPIRE: STRIKE ONE!

BEECHWOOD PITCHER: This next pitch is gonna have some extra spin on it!

SFX PERSON: BONK!

UMPIRE: Foul ball. STRIKE TWO!

NARRATOR: Now Herbie's sister was waving her hands in the air.

OLIVIA: YOU GOT A PIECE, HERBIE! You're up with the ball.

BEECHWOOD PITCHER: This batter is dead. I'm delivering strike three.

HERBIE: No you're not . . . I've gotta do this . . . the team is depending on me! I see that ball . . .

SFX PERSON: BLAM!

OLIVIA: Herbie got a hit! I knew he would! Just look at that ball zoom into right field!

UMPIRE: SAFE AT FIRST!

HERBIE: YAAAAHOOOOOO!

MR. and MRS. JONES: THAT'S MY SON!

LAUREL BEEF TEAM: (Cheer! Clap.)

UNCLE DWIGHT: Herbie brought Margie home! It's a 2–1 ball game!

PHILLIP: And it's the top of the batting order. *Annabelle's* up!

NARRATOR: The first baseman sat down on the field.

BEECHWOOD FIELDER: Might as well take a break. This girl takes *all day* at the plate.

ANNABELLE: (Clears throat.) First, knee bends. Second, deep breathing exercises. (Inhales and exhales several times.) Third, stretch the bat over my head. Tap the dirt from my cleats. And now, I will take my batting stance and a few practice swings.

BEECHWOOD FIELDER: (Yawns.) I can't believe it. She's finally ready.

BEECHWOOD PITCHER: I'm winding up. Here comes lightning!

UMPIRE: STRIKE ONE.

MR. HODGEKISS: Hey! That was so low night crawlers could have gotten it!

ANNABELLE: (Holds up her hand.) It's okay, Dad. I just have to make a small adjustment.

BEECHWOOD FIELDER: *Now* what is she doing?

ANNABELLE: I forgot to line up my knuckles on the bat.

BEECHWOOD FIELDER: (Shakes head.) That girl's a *real* doozie!

NARRATOR: When the pitcher threw the next ball, it was high and down the middle. Annabelle attacked it!

SFX PERSON: CRACK!

ANNABELLE: I'm ripping this ball into center field.

HERBIE: I'm rounding second and coming home! YEEEEEHAW!

UNCLE DWIGHT: WAY TO GO, BIG BEEF! Herbie's run makes it a tied ball game!

LAUREL BEEF TEAM: BIG BEEF! BIG BEEF! BIG BEEF!

ANNABELLE: DAD, I GOT A TRIPLE AND AN RBI!

MR. HODGEKISS: ALL RIGHT! Way to go, Annie! Now, *you're* the winning run! Be ready for the coach's signal to come home.

NARRATOR: Phillip put his glove on his head.

PHILLIP: I don't believe it! We have a chance to win this game. Who's up?

UNCLE DWIGHT: Ray Mart's up.

PHILLIP: YEAH! He got two hits today. (Pauses.) Where is he?

UNCLE DWIGHT: I see him. He just bought a chili dog at the refreshment stand. RAY MART, GET OVER HERE!

RAY MART: (Eating.) Mmmmmmmmmm. Man, this dog is good.

PHILLIP: What a slob. The guy's got chili all over his hands. Eweyee . . . now there's chili on his bat.

UNCLE DWIGHT: All right, Ray. We need you to hit Annabelle home.

RAY MART: (Gulps and licks lips.) Okay, I'm feelin' good.

NARRATOR: Ray took a low swing and hit a foul ball. As it rolled by the Laurel Beef bench, everyone groaned.

JOHN: Eweyee, look! Ray got chili on the ball!

LAUREL BEEF TEAM: GROSS!

UMPIRE: STRIKE ONE.

HERBIE: Ray's not concentrating. He's gone back to his old style of hitting.

UNCLE DWIGHT: Come on, Ray Mart. *Level* swing.

NARRATOR: Ray wasn't paying attention. He took another golf swing at the next pitch.

SFX PERSON: BONK!

HERBIE: Ray hit a nubber!

JOHN: Look! It just dribbled out halfway to the pitcher's mound and stopped.

UNCLE DWIGHT: GO, RAY! COME ON HOME, ANNABELLE!

ANNABELLE: I'm coming, Coach!

NARRATOR: Ray took off for first base while the pitcher charged the ball.

ANNABELLE: This is going to be close!

PHILLIP: I'm covering my eyes.

ANNABELLE: Look out, catcher! I'm sliding home—feet first!

HERBIE: The pitcher has the ball now. He's tossing it home!

NARRATOR: Annabelle's braids went high in the air as she started her slide.

ANNABELLE: I'm hitting the dirrrrrrrrrrt!

HERBIE: What a cloud of dust!

JOHN: Who got there first? The ball or Annabelle? I can't see.

PHILLIP: I don't wanna see!

NARRATOR: Everyone but Phillip looked at the umpire as the cloud of dust finally settled.

UMPIRE: SAFE!

LAUREL BEEF TEAM: YAAAAAHOOOOOOOOOOOOOOO!

PHILLIP: (Uncovers eyes.) I KNEW IT ALL ALONG!

UNCLE DWIGHT: Okay, Beefers, let's go get the nubber king and put him on our shoulders. We're going to the refreshment stand. My treat!

NARRATOR: The team cheered as they followed their coach to first base and lifted Ray in the air.

TEAM: RAY MART! RAY MART! RAY MART!

NARRATOR: As they carried Ray across the field, the coach put up his hand to stop the chant.

UNCLE DWIGHT: Just one thing, Ray . . . I always told you, you have to have something on the ball, but I didn't mean chili.

LAUREL BEEF TEAM: (Laughs.)

UNCLE DWIGHT: TO THE REFRESHMENT STAND!

RAY MART: (Puts fist in the air.) *Hot dog!*

HIRAM HALLE MEM. (POUND RIDGE)

3 1026 15024784 7

J
812.5
K

Kline, Suzy.
    The Herbie Jones Reader's
Theater.

Hiram Halle Memorial Library
Pound Ridge, New York